A SEQUEL TO *THE ICON EFFECT*

THE
TAKEO
EFFECT

HOW A BILLIONAIRE
SAMURAI WARRIOR
SAVED MY LIFE...

DARREN SUGIYAMA

Publisher's Note:
The characters and events in this book are merely fictional.

This book is dedicated to:

My mother for giving me life…

Bob & Charlene for saving my life…

My wife Emilia for changing my life…

and to my son Estevan for making my life worth living.

Table Of Contents

Chapter 1: Peaceful Journey…………………………..... pg. 7

Chapter 2: Going Back To Cali.................................. pg. 15

Chapter 3: The Wrath Of Kane........................... pg. 23

Chapter 4: When Two Tribes Go To War...................... pg. 35

Chapter 5: Landslide …………................................ pg. 45

Chapter 6: I Need A Doctor ……………................. pg. 61

Chapter 7: No New Friends……………................... pg. 67

Chapter 8: Still……………................................. pg. 75

Chapter 9: Titanium………………………….pg. 83

Chapter 10: A Change Is Gonna Come...................... pg. 101

Chapter 11: I'm Still Standing…………................ pg. 115

Chapter 12: The Light………………................ pg. 127

Chapter 13: Know The Ledge…………................ pg. 139

Chapter 14: Going The Distance………………….. pg. 153

Chapter 15: Gonna Fly Now…………................ pg. 165

Chapter 16: Loyalty, Loyalty, Loyalty……………...pg. 171

Chapter 17: Behind Bars……………................ pg. 181

Chapter 18: The Cycle………...………................ pg. 197

Chapter 1
Peaceful Journey

It was still dark outside.

I sat there, early in the morning, slouched on the opulent velvet sofa in the massive living room of my mother-in-law's house. My laptop computer stared at me, but I lacked the courage to stare back at it. Well, maybe I glanced at it a few times. I fell asleep just before midnight and only slept for a few hours before waking up filled with anxiety. I was emotionally exhausted, yet the combination of adrenaline and trepidation was enough to keep my eyelids open – barely open. I tried my best to change my blank stare from the huge rustic beams that ran across the 20-foot high ceilings back to my computer screen, but I just couldn't seem to force myself to do it.

We always stayed at my mother-in-law Isabella's home when we came to Los Angeles. Whether we were there for business or a vacation, it always became a family affair. As I continued to sit there in the dark by myself, my wife Valentina quietly walked into the room.

"Honey, do you know what time it is?" she asked.

"Umm, no. No, I uh… I don't," I murmured as I continued to stare at the ceiling.

"Babe, it's three o'clock in the morning. It's going to be a long day today and you need to get some rest. Come back to bed," Valentina said as she gently kissed me on the forehead.

In an exhausted and distracted voice, I said, "I can't sleep… and I have to prepare for my talk today. I still don't know exactly what I'm going to say."

I certainly didn't lack content, but for the first time in a long time, I felt completely unprepared. I didn't know where to begin. I started developing the framework of this talk weeks ago, but every time I attempted to author my thoughts, I found myself going off on tangents, none of which properly expressed the points I wanted to

7

articulate. This morning was no different as almost two hours had passed. My bloodshot eyes burned as they now stared at my blank laptop screen. The little mouse pointer kept blinking at me, urging me to author something magnificent, but every time I started typing, I found myself hitting the delete button as many times as my other keystrokes.

I wrote my book – *The Icon Effect* – so easily, as if I was the beneficiary of some sort of divine inspiration, yet there I sat with so many things to say and no words on my laptop's screen. It was now 4:53 a.m. and I still had nothing. I decided to make myself an Americano, hoping the caffeine would potentially spark some literary inspiration. As I held the warm ceramic coffee mug in my hands, I reminisced over the many evenings I spent with my mentor – The Icon – in this very room talking about the future – *our* future. The Icon was such an amazing mentor to me. To think that I was his protégé-turned-son-in-law made me believe in miracles. I missed him so much, and while I was grateful for the time I got to spend with him, I felt incomplete without him.

It had been just over a decade since The Icon passed away, and though I enjoyed my fabulous lifestyle – a lifestyle that was funded by the company he gave me – I often thought about where my happiness truly came from. For so long, I yearned for financial success, thinking that achievements and accolades would bring me happiness. But over time, I found that my happiness had very little to do with the *things* I had acquired, and more to do with the man I had become in the process.

"Perhaps this could be the foundation of my talk today," I thought to myself.

I had so many stories to share about how The Icon and Joseph had helped me become not just a *wealthy* man, but a *better* man. I certainly had no shortage of inventory in that regard. These two men literally changed my life.

"Good morning Papa," my nine-year old son Cortez softly mumbled as he entered the dark living room, curling up next to me on the sofa.

"It's still really early buddy. You should go back to sleep. It's going to be a long day today," I said, realizing this was the same thing Valentina told me two hours earlier.

"Nah, I'm good Papa. Can I just snuggle with you?"

"Of course pal. You can always snuggle with me," I said, motioning him to come join me on the sofa.

Cortez snuggled up next to me, leaning against my left arm, making it impossible to type on my computer. Valentina had taught me to soak in these moments – to take time to smell the roses – for moments like these are lost forever once they have passed.

She would often tell me, "Vincent, there will be nights and early mornings where our son will want you to hold him, and even when you're sleep-deprived and want to be left alone, remember that one day Cortez will reach an age where he won't want that kind of affection from you anymore."

She always reminded me to relish such moments. These types of lessons were clearly taught to Valentina by her parents – The Icon and Isabella. I learned that the lessons that parents teach their children have multi-generational ripple effects. I was certainly the beneficiary The Icon's mentorship, but the blessing of being married to someone that could remind me of these principles when I needed them the most was a perfect example of that multi-generational ripple effect.

We had planned on having more children, but after several attempts and two miscarriages after Cortez, Valentina and I decided to count our blessings and be grateful for our one-and-only son. Instead of getting depressed about not being able to have more children, it just made us even more grateful of the one we were blessed with.

Often times we have a picture in our minds of what we want our lives to become, and sometimes these expectations lead us to having feelings of entitlement. But I felt entitled to nothing, for entitlement is the architect of disappointment and resentment. I had always worried that something might go wrong with Valentina's pregnancy when she was pregnant with Cortez, so when he was born a healthy baby, I literally broke down in tears right there in the delivery room. He was more than I ever dreamed of. I was so grateful for our son's health, for I was acutely aware of everything that can go wrong during childbirth, both for the baby and for the delivering mother.

Having two miscarriages was difficult for us to go through, and the last miscarriage put Valentina's life in danger. Miscarriages are so common, yet people rarely ever talk about having them. I think this really does aspiring mothers a disservice. I have heard that so many women experience feelings of depression, guilt, and unworthiness when they experience a miscarriage, mostly because they feel like they're the only one experiencing the inability to carry their baby to term. But the reality is, I know very few mothers that haven't had at least one miscarriage.

I thought to myself, "Perhaps this should be the theme of my talk today, that living more transparently regarding our own struggles can console and empower others going through similar challenges, letting them know that they're not alone."

"No, that's too personal to share," I told myself.

Just then, Cortez whispered, "Papa, can you hold me?"

I put down my computer for a moment and held my son close. He wrapped his legs so intertwined with mine, we looked like a giant human pretzel. These were the moments Valentina told me to soak in, for one day, these moments would be gone forever. We both fell back asleep on the sofa. My alarm finally sounded off at 6:00 a.m. and I still had nothing prepared for my talk that day – no well-articulated speech to read, no notes, and not a hint of progress.

I told myself that perhaps it would be better to just speak from the heart. The Icon once shared with me that some of his best speeches were not speeches at all, but rather organic intimate fireside chats that just so happened to be in front of a group of several hundred people. Maybe my talk was meant to be one of these *Icon-style* fireside chats, but despite how much I tried to convince myself of this, my unpreparedness made me feel like I was disrespecting the importance of the event. Even more importantly,

I felt I was disrespecting the people that asked me to speak at it, for being chosen was truly an honor.

It was an overcast Los Angeles morning, and although *The Hotel 100* was only a few minutes from Isabella's home, on this particular morning, it felt like a journey to get there. As our driver pulled up to the valet, Valentina smiled at me and asked, "Are you ready?"

I knew her question was in reference to a multitude of things. I just smiled at her with a very unconvincing smile, knowing that I was neither prepared nor *ready*. She smiled back, giving me her signature reassuring grin that she always gave me when she knew I needed it.

The lobby of *The Hotel 100* was beautifully decorated. Francisco's new protégés were all up front, greeting the guests as they arrived. After The Icon passed away, Francisco – his adopted son – inherited the remaining shares of the hotel. It had always been his pride and joy, for he built this empire alongside his adoptive father during his entire adult life. I had so many fond memories of working at the hotel in the early stages of my career as Francisco's apprentice, but today, Francisco would not be working the event. He would be sitting in the front row.

As the program began, I sat up straight in my chair, staring at the ground as I bit my bottom lip with apprehension. I felt Valentina's reassuring hand placed upon mine, but for the most part, I was lost in a world of my own as my mind raced, trying to gather my composure and formulate what I was going to say. I was still neither prepared nor *ready*.

"Next up, Vincent Montgomery will say a few words," said Pastor Curtis, awakening me out of my trance.

I slowly walked up to the stage, still not knowing exactly what I was going to say. I adjusted the microphone as I stood behind the podium, clearing my throat several times. As I looked at the crowd, I felt like things began to move in slow motion. I could feel my heart rate slowly decrease, the way a record player sounds when someone pulls the power plug. I slowly inhaled with uncertainty – held my breath for a split second – then released a long stuttering exhale.

As I surveyed the giant banquet room, it was filled with some of the most influential power players in the financial world, but the most important people were sitting in the front row – Isabella, Valentina and Cortez, Francisco and his brothers and sister and their spouses, but no Andrei.

I attempted to clear my throat again a few times as I looked down at Valentina. She gave me her signature reassuring smile again, nodding her head as if to say, "You've got this. Just speak from the heart."

I took another sip from the bottle of water I placed on the shelf under the podium and began.

"Many years ago, I walked into a high-rise building not far from here. I was told by my new mentor – The Icon – that I was going to meet the Managing Partner of his wealth management firm for a 7:00 a.m. meeting, and that I was going to start my internship working for him. Out of the conference room walked a man that looked like a real-life superhero to me. He greeted me as if I was a member of the club, and over time, he became part of my family… or more accurately, *I* became part of *his* family. His name was Joseph Balmain," I said, taking another deep breath to calm my nerves.

I fought to hold back tears, but it was too late. They were already streaming down my cheeks.

I continued, "I was magnificently mentored by The Icon himself, but Joseph… Joseph was my day-to-day mentor. He gave me the constant encouragement I needed back when I was just getting started in my career with The Icon. And even after I moved out to New York while they were both out here in Los Angeles, my daily phone conversations with Joseph made me feel like my big brother was sitting right by my side. When I received the news that his jet crashed and that his entire family perished – he, Christine and his sons – it felt like the wind had been knocked out of me."

Joseph and his family were on vacation in Barbados. The details of what went wrong on that flight still had not been determined, but I didn't care about the details. I didn't want to know the details. I had now lost my second mentor – second to The Icon. As I recounted my most precious memories with this great man, sharing them with the rest of the mourning guests at the service, my eulogy became more of tribute to someone I always aspired to emulate. There were too many amazing stories to share all of them, and no one story was any more precious than the other. They were all invaluable to me.

Joseph not only taught me how to excel as a great leader and businessman, but also how to excel as a better father and husband. What made Joseph great was not his power, wealth, or status, but rather it was his humility and the way he loved his wife. It was the way he loved his sons. It was the way he loved me.

Though Joseph was a masterful teacher, the most important lessons he taught me were not through instruction. They were taught to me through his example. Just watching the way he treated people – not only his family and his business associates, but everyone he came into contact with – was a masterclass in humility and kindness. As I said, he didn't just teach me to be a *wealthier* man. He taught me to be a *better* man.

As I wrapped up my tribute, I looked at the beautiful picture of Joseph's family that was displayed on the right side of the stage and said, "Joseph, thank you for being such an amazing big brother to me and welcoming me into your family. You looked like a superhero to me when you first walked out of that conference room, and you've never stopped looking like a superhero to me ever since that day."

As I walked off the stage, pausing to take one final look at the picture of Joseph and his family, I whispered in a trembling voice, "I'm going to miss you big brother. I wish you a peaceful journey."

Chapter 2
Going Back To Cali

I was now flying back and forth from New York to Los Angeles every other week, taking over Joseph's responsibilities at the firm in Beverly Hills. It was exhausting, but I wore that responsibility on my sleeve as a badge of honor. Valentina and Cortez always flew with me, which in many ways was nice because we got to see Isabella more often. Valentina was home schooling Cortez during that time which made our frequent family commutes to the West Coast possible, but over the next several months, it had become very apparent that commuting coast to coast was neither a practical nor an enjoyable way for a young family to live long-term.

Four years ago, Kane – the young man I met at *Madre's Coffee* – relocated to New York City to become my intern. I also hired him as my driver, providing him with some part-time income during his unpaid internship. I took him to lunch every day and tried to help him financially in any way I could without removing the sweat equity required to succeed at my firm. I wanted to mentor Kane the way The Icon and Joseph had mentored me. He was driven and hungry, and did whatever I told him to do. I had personally mentored Kane over the last four years, and to no one's surprise except his own, he became the top revenue-generating advisor at my firm.

One evening, I invited him over for dinner at our home to discuss our next moves. As dinner came to an end, I said, "I'd like to propose a toast. Kane, you've come a long way since we first met at *Madre's Coffee* shop years ago in Los Angeles, and you've certainly lived up to the origin of your name. You are indeed a *battler.*"

Kane smiled, slightly blushing.

"With my responsibilities of running both our New York office, as well as our Beverly Hills office, it's beginning to take a toll on our family. Cortez is starting fourth grade next year, so Valentina and I have decided to relocate our family to Los Angeles, and I want you to run our New York office. I'm offering you a new position Kane. Managing Partner."

"Oh my God Vincent! Are you serious?" Kane exclaimed.

"You've really come a long way. In fact, you remind me of a young, hungry kid that met The Icon in the same coffee shop you met me at. That kid was really rough around the edges, and he had no experience whatsoever, but The Icon took a chance on him, and it paid off… for everyone," I said.

Kane knew that scrappy young kid I was referring to was me. The circumstances were so similar but there were several significant differences. One, the age gap between Kane and me was much less than it was between me and The Icon. Two, the level of success The Icon had achieved when we first met far surpassed what I had achieved when I met Kane. And three, The Icon was so much wiser than I was at this point in my life. I still had much to learn, and with my two main mentors having passed away, I knew I had a long road of personal and professional development ahead of me. I would have to learn new lessons the hard way by making mistakes and self-correcting them along the way. I was nervous about letting Kane run the New York office while I relocated my family to California, but I knew it was a necessary move. Joseph was such a hands-on leader that his mere presence in the office created a certain energy, and in his absence, I knew I would have to fulfill his role in that capacity in the Beverly Hills office.

We began looking at homes in Beverly Hills and Brentwood, as well as high-rise penthouses along the Wilshire Corridor. I was so used to the New York City lifestyle that high-rise living had grown on me, but Valentina and I thought Cortez might enjoy having a big backyard. He absolutely loved going to his grandma Isabella's house and running around the enormous property.

One evening after Valentina had put Cortez to sleep, she came into the living room with two flutes of sipping tequila – *Siete Leguas*, blanco. This was my new favorite tequila. She handed me one of the flutes – served *neat*, just as I liked it – and said, "Okay, so… I have something to ask you," with a mischievous grin.

Valentina had several signature grins – as many as there are shades of orange in a sunset – and each one told a significantly different story.

"Okaaaay," I curiously replied, wondering what kind of fabulous proposition my wife had conjured up in her adventurous mind.

"So I was talking to Mama, and, umm… if you don't want to do it, I'll understand, okay… but uhh… she uhh… she asked what we thought about the idea of instead of buying a house in Los Angeles… that we, uhh… you know, maybe move in with her. If you don't want to do it, I'll understand, but uhh… what do you think about that?" she hesitantly inquired.

I started laughing hysterically. I knew Valentina so well. One of her most admirable qualities was the pride she carried of doing things on her own – something we shared in common – something we bonded over so deeply. She knew that my pride might prevent me from living in a house that I didn't buy myself, but I learned that my ego was far less important than what was best for my family. It would be amazing for Cortez to grow up with his *abuela* living in the same house. It would also be great for Isabella to spend that kind of time with her grandson as well. She adored him so much. He was, after all, her only biological grandchild. But I also understood the special bond that Valentina had with her mother, and I knew this was something that would make her happy.

I was at the point in my life where I didn't need *privacy*. I wanted my family *close*. If you had asked me back when I was single if I'd want to live in the same house as my mother-in-law once I was married, I would have laughed hysterically, for that would have sounded like the worst thing ever. But with Isabella specifically, and with my wife and son specifically, I felt it would be magical.

"Honey, I'm in," I said, smiling with ultimate certainty.

"Really! Are you sure you'd be okay with this? I mean, I know it's not what you envisioned, and I mean, it might not be ideal for you because I know you like your privacy sometimes… but… are you sure? Are you really sure?" Valentina asked, the way a child asks if it's okay for them to open their Christmas presents on Christmas Eve instead of Christmas morning.

I burst into laughter again, reassuring her that I was totally onboard with this arrangement. I can't explain it, but everything about this move felt *right*. I called Isabella the very next day to talk about the details of our soon-to-be new living situation.

"Vincent, thank you so much for doing this. I know this isn't what you had in mind – moving in with your mother-in-law – but I assure you, you will have your privacy. I even thought about redecorating our guest house so you can have a *man cave* all to yourself if you want to get away from me to get some work done, or even to just relax and enjoy a nice cocktail with a friend or a business associate," Isabella told me.

But as I said, I didn't need privacy at this point in my life. Plus, the mere scale of her house was more than enough to provide privacy anyway. It was a beautiful Spanish-style hacienda in Bel Air – 18,000 square feet with twelve bedrooms – and was a place that was very special to me, for it was where my original mentor built his life with his family.

When Isabella told me about converting the guest house into a *man cave* for me, though I appreciated it, it was so unnecessary. The guest house was a beautiful 5,000 square foot, four-bedroom mini-hacienda. To think I used to refer to a living space that large as being a *mini-anything* still makes me laugh.

The move was relatively easy. There wasn't much to ship to Isabella's house since we were keeping our New York apartment, and because I would be frequently traveling back to the East Coast for business, I needed to keep it fully furnished with a full wardrobe there anyway.

Isabella arranged for her driver to pick us up from LAX upon our arrival that afternoon. We only had a few suitcases of clothing because Valentina planned to outfit everyone in our family with a new wardrobe for our new West Coast home. When we arrived at Isabella's, she had a beautiful lunch prepared for us under the pavilion, poolside. She was so happy to see us, and even happier that our family would all be living under one roof.

As her personal assistant was arranging our outdoor table, Isabella pulled me aside and said, "Vincent, I want you to know that I consider this *our* home now – not *my* home – *our* home. You're the man of this house now, and I never want you to feel like a *guest* here. I know this living arrangement will take some getting used to – for us to find our rhythm together – but it's important to me that you feel as comfortable here as you would in a home you bought yourself."

Isabella motioned me to follow her as we walked to the other side of the massive property to the guest house. It was a magnificent structure that was rarely ever used. We entered the rustic alder wood front door and walked over to the living room. It's décor had a unique modern Mexican flair with a Southwestern appeal, yet also incorporated splashes of Colombian elements to honor Isabella's culture. A collection of vintage *sombrero vueltiaos* – traditional Colombian hats woven out of cane leaves – hung from the living room wall above the low slung white linen sofa Isabella asked me to join her on.

"My husband originally had this casita built for my mother with the expectation that she would one day leave Colombia and join us, but that never happened, so we rarely ever used it. But for extremely important business meetings where he wanted a more intimate setting than his Beverly Hills office, this was where he held those special meetings. He said it magically disarmed people and made them feel more comfortable with him. There's something special about inviting someone into your home that creates a higher level of trust than just meeting with them in a conference room in a sterile commercial office building, and to have a space like this that is on your own property, yet separate from your main house, is the perfect combination of personal intimacy and business focus. I want you to use this casita the same way my husband once did," Isabella explained.

Again, to call a 5,000 square foot structure a *casita* was quite the understatement.

"Vincent, I told Valentina that this would be *your* space. Not *our* space, but *your* space. I want you to have a space that you can escape to when you need to. Whether it's writing your next book, or a special business meeting you want to have away from your office, this is where you can do that, okay?" Isabella said, smiling in an attempt to make me feel autonomous.

She continued, "Tomorrow morning I have three different interior designers coming over, and I want you to meet with each of them separately and pick the one you like the best, and you can redecorate this place however you want. This is my little gift to you for making my dream come true of having my daughter and grandson under one roof with me."

"Isabella, I feel like *I* should be the one giving *you* a gift for allowing us to move into your beautiful home like this."

She immediately cut me off, correcting my verbal blunder.

"No! *Our* home. Not *my* home. *Our* home!" Isabella said, jokingly scolding me for my real estate miscategorization.

"Okay, okay. *Our* home," I said, correcting myself.

"That's more like it. The first one will be here at nine o'clock tomorrow morning, and I spaced them one hour apart, so after you've met with each of them, you can let me know which one you like, and I'll set up the rest, okay?"

"Isabella, that's incredibly generous of you, but I want to keep it exactly the way it is, if that's okay with you. If this is the way The Icon designed it, then this is the way it's supposed to be," I said, expecting her to revere my sentiment, but instead, she started laughing hysterically.

"He didn't design it this way! I did!" Isabella exclaimed, lovingly slapping me on my thigh.

"Well in that case, even more so. Please call those designers and cancel the appointments. I want this place to look exactly as you originally designed it," I said.

Isabella acquiesced, and by the way she looked at me, I could tell that my request to keep the interior décor untouched secretly pleased her, knowing that I valued nostalgia as much as she did.

But there was something I had to know.

"If The Icon held some of his most important meetings here, why didn't he ever do that with me?" I curiously asked.

Isabella smiled as she looked at me with her loving eyes saying, "Vincent, my husband never met with you in the guest house because he never viewed you as a *guest*. He viewed you as *family* from the very beginning. Do you remember all the dinners we had in our dining room together, and all the late night chats you had with him in our living room over a nice bottle of tequila? Guess how many other business people he met with in our home like that. Other than Joseph and Andrei, it was just you. Our main house was reserved for family only. You were part of his inner circle from the very beginning. He told me that when he first met you, he felt like being your mentor was part of his destiny."

Even years after The Icon's passing, I continued to learn just how special a man he really was. I was lucky to have known such a man. After we finished our conversation, Isabella and I walked out of the guest house to join the others for lunch. As we walked across the property, I put my arm around Isabella and said, "It will be an honor to use this guest house – the same place that was used by my mentor – but more importantly, because it was designed by you, mom."

That was the first time I had ever called Isabella *mom*. I don't know why I had never called her that before. Perhaps it was my way of subconsciously honoring my own mom – a way of reserving that special title for someone that had loved me so much – someone that I loved so much. Just as Isabella promised to make sure I had the privacy I needed, it turned out that I neither needed nor wanted any privacy, and though we were already *family*, we were now a family that lived under one roof.

My business trips to New York now became solo missions as my family stayed behind in Los Angeles. We enrolled Cortez in a private school in Beverly Hills, and Valentina's days of home school teaching came to an end. Though she never complained about it, I know it was somewhat of a relief for her to step out of that role and just focus on being a mother and co-running our household with Isabella. Knowing that Isabella was there to help Valentina with Cortez gave me peace of mind, though I knew

Valentina didn't *need* help with anything. She had home schooled Cortez for the first, second, and third grade and had a level of teaching skills that was beyond human. But of course she was a great teacher, for she was the daughter of the greatest teacher ever – The Icon.

In many ways, Joseph's death and our residential relocation to the West Coast brought our family even closer together. We were able to spend so much more time with Isabella, and I got to see Francisco more often as well. I learned to search for the silver lining in every tragedy in pursuit of discovering the collateral beauty. Without this ability, tragedies and struggles in life can destroy a person, but having the perspective and ability to reframe these hardships contextualizes them, giving you power over them instead of *them* having power over *you*. Instead of allowing myself to feel like a victim due to the challenges and curveballs life threw at me, I trained myself to look at them as opportunities to grow as a person.

I was taught so many lessons by my mentors – The Icon, Joseph, and Francisco – and it was my duty to pass these lessons down to Kane, my protégé. It was a way for me to honor my own mentors and perpetuate The Icon's legacy. My mentors always viewed our inner circle as more than just business associates and friends, but instead as *family*, and it was now time for me to induct the most recent addition into our family – my new *little brother*, Kane.

Chapter 3
The Wrath Of Kane

There is something sacred about the bond between a mentor and his mentee. When I think back to how The Icon, Joseph, and Francisco mentored me, they literally changed the course of my life, forever.

I had played the role of a mentor to dozens of my employees, but it was now time to develop my first team captain from ground zero, the same way my mentors developed me from ground zero. I had big plans for Kane and hoped that one day he would become my successor.

On my trips to New York to help Kane transition into his new role as *Managing Partner* of the firm, I often reminisced over something Joseph taught me years ago. On the first day of my internship with Joseph, he explained to me, "Vincent, one day you're going to refer to these early days of struggle as your *Good Old Days*, so never forget what this feels like right now. Never forget how nervous you are right now – the feelings of anxiety, worry, and fear – because one day when you're a successful leader, you're going to have the same talk I'm having with you... but the difference is that you'll be in my position, and you'll have to encourage a young, new protégé and tell them stories about your *Good Ole Days*. If you can remember exactly how you feel right now, your people will be able to relate to you. They'll aspire to be like you, but more importantly, they'll believe that with your guidance, they can be successful too. You need to instill the belief in them that if you did it, then maybe they can do it too."

Every time I thought about that conversation with Joseph, my eyes would fill up with tears. I remember exactly how I felt on the first day of my internship, consumed by the utter fear that I didn't belong in this new world. But despite this near paralyzing fear, Joseph painted a picture of me one day being in his position, and that alone gave me the glimpse of hope I needed to believe it was all possible.

Like every mentor-in-training, Kane struggled with the frustrations of not being able to get 100% of our new employees to march in unison to the beat of his drum. He would explicitly lay out our process to these young advisors, but he lacked the patience that being a mentor requires.

I remember my own lack of patience when I was first learning how to become a mentor – the frustration of wanting someone to succeed so badly that I almost wanted it for them more than they wanted it for themselves. It is an emotional investment that requires the most altruistic intentions, but also requires masterful planning the way a chess master sets up his every move fifteen moves in advance. Kane and I would spend hours together, game planning, debriefing, and talking about the future – *our* future. Though our age difference was one of a big-brother-to-little-brother, he was more like a son to me. It was a beautiful relationship.

There were times where Kane and I would be in deep conversation and my son Cortez would call me on the phone to say goodnight. Though I always took Cortez's call, often times I would rush to end the call with my own son just so I could get back to my mentoring sessions with Kane. I am embarrassed to admit this, but in my enthusiasm to mentor Kane, I often times neglected the emotional needs of my own son. Though I knew Joseph would have never made this mistake with his sons, and that The Icon would have never done this with Valentina, there was something intoxicating about being regarded by Kane as highly as I regarded Joseph and The Icon. I remember New Year's Eve that year, I was at Isabella's house with my family when I received a text from Kane.

"Vincent, while everyone else is out partying tonight, I decided to stay at home. I'm sitting in my living room right now reflecting on the last four years of my life and how much you've given to me. You're the big brother I never had. Thank you for everything you're doing for me. I love you. -Kane."

It was acknowledgements like this that made me feel like my life was relevant. It fulfilled me in a way that was more precious than money, awards, or any success I may have achieved. The Icon always told me that the gift of giving was for the giver, and as thankful as I was for the gift he gave me, I now understood what he meant. It was so much more fulfilling to impact someone else's life than it was to become successful myself.

This was *The Icon Effect*.

On my next trip to New York, I had my assistant Julia arrange an event to celebrate Kane's success and formally introduce him as the new *Managing Partner* of my New York office. We rented out an entire restaurant in Soho, hired a DJ, and invited all our employees and their spouses. I even invited Andrei and gave him *carte blanche* to invite whomever he felt would liven up the party. In true *Andrei fashion*, he invited just about every aspiring supermodel in New York City.

It was a way to commemorate this momentous time in Kane's life, garnering indisputable acknowledgement that he would now be our new East Coast leader. We popped champagne bottle after champagne bottle that night, toasting Kane over and over. Though this type of flashy party scene wasn't Valentina's scene, she understood the aspirational brand we were building. Kane was our *brand ambassador*, symbolizing what was possible as we attempted to motivate all the young guns we recruited to our firm. To have someone as young as Kane running the show sent a message to all of these young advisors that if Kane could rise to the top this fast, then it was possible for them too.

Andrei poured even more gasoline on the fire by wearing more diamond jewelry than *Slick Rick* and *Liberace* combined, showing up with three very scantily clad Brazilian girls tending to his every need that night. Even though Kane would always tell me that he wanted a family-oriented life like mine, I could tell that Andrei's flashy single life was alluring to him. I suppose I couldn't blame him. When I first moved to New York City, Andrei's flashy lifestyle intrigued me too. His over-the-top style was coveted by any young man searching to fill his inner void with symbols of power.

25

"Yo Kane, come over and join us lil homie! Alessandra wants to meet you!" Andrei said, motioning him to sit with him on the sofa with his Brazilian lingerie model entourage.

Andrei laughed out loud in his slightly arrogant and obnoxious way as he winked at me. It reminded me of my old single days when I first moved to New York, back when Andrei used to take me out clubbing with him. One of the girls – Alessandra – sat on Kane's lap in her tiny little barely-there dress, flirting with him like a *professional*. I don't know if Andrei's entourage was on his payroll, but they certainly acted like they were *paid attendees*. Though they certainly amplified the excitement that evening, Valentina and I were not fans of this mildly inappropriate display of public affection.

Kane and Andrei seemed to really hit it off that evening, and though Andrei brought certain elements of distraction into Kane's life, I do remember how comforting it was for me to have Andrei as my wingman during my assimilation into single life in NYC. Their interaction made me feel slightly uncomfortable, but I figured that was just a sign of me getting old. I was once young and single too, and I understood Kane's fascination with Andrei's *high life*.

Valentina and I stood across the room talking to several of our employees getting to know their spouses, but I knew Valentina's discerning eye was aware of Andrei's antics the entire evening. Overall, the event was a big success, but I could tell that Valentina was not entirely pleased. She felt like Andrei intentionally made a spectacle of himself to gain the attention of our young male employees, which he certainly succeeded at doing. We stayed until the end of the event, and as our last guests departed, Valentina and I quickly debriefed with my assistant Julia.

"You sure know how to throw one heck of a party, Vincent!" Julia said.

"Yeah, I think people had a good time, especially Kane. And did you see how excited our new young employees were? If this doesn't motivate them to work harder, man, I don't know!" I said, feeling like this couldn't have been a better marketing event for the firm.

"Where's Kane? I haven't seen him for a while," I asked.

"He left early with Andrei," she replied.

"Really? He didn't even say goodbye."

In a conflicted and troubled voice, Julia said, "Well that's disappointing. He looked a little out of it towards the end. His eyes were pretty dilated too. I didn't want to say anything, but I thought you should know. I saw him and Andrei and those three... uh... girls... come out of the men's restroom together and they looked like... well... like they were partying a little too hard if you know what I mean. I didn't know if I should tell you this Vincent. I didn't want to upset you at an event like this."

"No, no, no. I'm glad you did Julia. Thank you. I'll talk to Kane about this tomorrow. Again, thank you for helping me put this event together Julia. I couldn't have done it without you. You're the best," I said, as our two drivers texted me, informing me that they were waiting for us curbside in front of the restaurant.

We walked out to our two black SUVs, and as I opened the door for Julia, Valentina gave her a hug, saying, "Thank you for being our eyes and ears all of these years Julia. My dad always said you were the one we could always trust. He really loved you."

Julia's eyes closed softly as she hugged Valentina saying, "He was such a good man. I miss him so much."

Julia worked for The Icon ever since she graduated from college over thirty years ago and had been a loyal employee ever since. Her daughter was attending the *NYU School of Law*, paid for by a trust account that The Icon had set up for her before his passing.

On the car ride back to our apartment that evening, Valentina asked me, "Honey, what did you think of Andrei bringing those girls to the event? Did you think that was appropriate?"

"I know, I know... it was a little embarrassing. Julia said some of the wives of our employees were a little upset too. I don't want them thinking that every time we have a company retreat and their husbands are away, that *this* is the environment we foster. I have to talk to Andrei about this, and Kane as well," I said, acknowledging Valentina's concerns.

"Thank you honey. I know how much you love Kane, and I know how proud of him you are. This was really thoughtful of you to throw this party for him. I just can't believe he took off without even saying thank you. Julia is right. It's disappointing," Valentina said.

"Hey, I agree. Maybe he just got caught up in the moment with Andrei. He did look like he was having the time of his life. We were once young and impressionable too… well, at least I was."

"Are you saying I'm old now?" Valentina asked, laughing as she poked me in the ribs.

"Baby, you're STILL young! I'm the old one!" I exclaimed.

"Nice recovery!" Valentina replied as she kissed me, reaching over to hold my hand.

The next day, Valentina flew back to Los Angeles, as I stayed behind in New York for a few more days. That next Monday, I called Andrei to talk to him about his antics that evening, but my call went straight to voicemail.

I left a message saying, "Andrei, this is Vincent. Hey, it was great seeing you the other night. It's been a while. But I have to talk to you about something I have some concerns about. Call me when you get a chance. Thanks buddy."

My flight was scheduled to take off that Monday evening, so Kane and I had an early dinner together. As we sat across from each other at the dinner table, we reviewed our plan for the week.

"That was some party Friday night, huh?" I said.

"Vincent, I'm sorry I didn't say goodbye that evening. I just got caught up with Andrei, and before I knew it, we were in his limousine with those three hot chicks. Honestly, I don't even remember how we got from the restaurant into the limo. It was weird because I didn't even drink that much. We ended up going back to Andrei's place, and from that moment on, all I remember is waking up at two o'clock in the afternoon the next day with that Alessandra chick and her friend in bed with me. I don't even remember what happened," Kane admitted.

"What do you mean you don't remember what happened?"

"It was like I blacked out for a few hours. I remember being at the restaurant, and I remember parts of the limo ride, but I don't remember how we even got up to Andrei's penthouse. I just woke up the next morning with those two hot chicks. It was weird," Kane said.

"Did you take anything that night?"

"What do you mean *take anything*?"

"Drugs. Did you take any drugs that evening?"

Kane looked downwards as he began fiddling with his dinner napkin. I could tell he was ashamed.

"Vincent, I've never done anything like this before. That Alessandra chick put a pill on her tongue and started kissing me with it in her mouth, and before I knew it, it was in my mouth, and from that moment on, I started feeling kinda funny," Kane said as he could no longer make eye contact with me.

"Kane, what were you thinking taking those girls into the bathroom with you at a company event? Do you understand how uncomfortable that made some of the wives of our employees seeing the five of you come out of the men's room together? Come on Kane, you know better than that," I said, showing visible signs of disappointment.

"I'm sorry Vincent. You're right. You have every right to be pissed at me. I've just never been the center of attention like that before, and that night, I felt like I was somebody important. You should have seen how pumped up our young employees got when they saw me with those two hot Brazilian chicks. They thought I was the man!"

"So getting two paid escorts to sleep with you makes you feel like you're *the man*?" I asked.

"Escorts? What do you mean?" Kane naively asked.

"Kane, those were clearly *working girls*. Why do you think they were all over you like that? Kane, part of my job is to perpetuate the legacy The Icon and Joseph passed down to me, and

I want to pass this gift down to you now, but I need to know I can trust you. Do you understand what I'm saying?" I asked.

"I do Vincent. I do. I'm sorry. I won't let it happen again, I promise. It kills me to know that I let you down, and I promise I'll make it up to you. I promise. I wish I could have met The Icon to tell him what an incredible mentor you've been to me. He would be so proud of you because... because you..."

Kane paused as his voice quivered. He looked at me with glassy eyes that were full of gratitude, and continued, "...because YOU have become MY icon. I love you Vincent," he said, standing up to hug me.

He hugged me the way a son hugs his father – in a firm yet tender way. It was the same way I used to hug The Icon.

On my flight from JFK back to LAX, I thought about what Kane shared with me, and it filled my heart. It reminded me of all the mistakes I made while learning from The Icon and Joseph, and how patient and forgiving they were with me. I remember Joseph telling me how many times he let The Icon down, yet The Icon's forgiveness and ability to help him find his *true north* just made their bond even stronger.

I tried my best to mentor Kane with the same level of forgiveness and understanding, believing that there is no sweeter journey for mentor than shepherding his protégé back to redemption when he has fallen, similar to the story of the *Prodigal Son*. I spent the next six months flying back and forth from coast to coast, continuing to mentor Kane through this huge career transition, and though it was exhausting for me, it gave me great pleasure to know that I was part of something that would honor my own mentors.

I always made a point to tell our employees how lucky they were to have Kane leading the charge. I even gave him credit for things he didn't actually do. I was fully aware that neither The Icon nor Joseph ever did this with me. I wanted to create a *mini-Vincent* so badly that I made excuses for Kane, covering up his shortcomings. I had put him up on a pedestal that he had not yet earned.

Over the next several months, I noticed that Kane would often times lose his temper with our employees, and even worse, with important people we had strong alliances with. Though his ego began to grow exponentially, I thought I would be able to coach him to maturity. But one time in particular, he crossed the line.

"Vincent, I'm not gonna let people talk down to me just because I'm young. That dude from *Zellan Capital* tried to come at me in our last board meeting, so I kicked him out of the conference room," Kane boasted.

"Kane, we've been doing business with *Zellan* for over twenty years. That was Davis Zellan – the grandson of their founder, Carter Zellan. Everyone knows he's a hot head. Sometimes you're going to have to take one on the chin with him. It's part of knowing how to manage that relationship. We need *Zellan* on our side," I explained.

"But he never talks to you like that. He always talks to you with respect," Kane argued.

"Yeah, you know why? It's because I make him feel like he's the most important person in the room. I let him be the *star*. We're in the business of making OTHER people feel important. And you know what happens when we do that? They fall in love with us. I can call his grandfather Carter on the phone right now and ask him for just about any favor, and it's done. I BUILT that kind of relationship with him over time. He knows his grandson is a pain in the butt. In fact, he tells me that all the time, but he also knows that I treat Davis like he's important, and because of that, Carter knows he owes me an infinite number of favors. But now that you kicked him out of our last board meeting, I have to go apologize to Carter. You let your big fat ego get in the way of business. You can't do that Kane," I scolded him.

The more I attempted to school up Kane on issues like this, the more defensive he got. It was clear that someone was planting seeds of resentment in Kane, but at that time, I didn't know who the devil sitting on his shoulder was.

When I returned to Los Angeles, I shared Kane's reaction to my mentoring with Valentina saying, "Babe, it was like talking to a completely different person this time. Every time I tried to teach him something, he pushed back, defending his position. His ego has gotten out of control."

"Honey, I hate to tell you this, but Kane just isn't ready. He lacks the maturity and social etiquette required to run the show. He doesn't understand that certain relationships require the *white glove treatment*, and he isn't mature enough to put his ego aside. I think he has potential, but he has a long way to go. He's no *Vincent Montgomery...* not in the least," Valentina lovingly told me.

She then said, "Look honey, just sleep on it and tomorrow you can make a decision on what to do. Maybe he just needs you to talk him through the mechanics on how to deal with these high-valued relationships again. He was probably just embarrassed that he let you down. Don't worry, babe. You'll figure it out. You always do."

The next morning, I thought about my interactions with Kane over the last several months. Though his countenance was far more combative and less appreciative on this last trip, I figured it was just the pressure of his new position that had him out of rhythm, for this was surely not the same Kane that once gushed over how much I had changed his life. Just then, Valentina walked into my office unexpectedly.

I said, "Hey honey! What I nice surprise! I thought you were golfing at Terranea today with Leticia."

"I was, but I cancelled," she said.

"Oh, is everything okay?"

"Vincent, I need to show you something important," she said in a stern tone of voice.

She closed the door to my office and began pacing back and forth in front of my desk, and I could tell she was infuriated about something. It wasn't in Valentina's nature to lose her temper, but I could tell she was about to explode. I had never seen her so visibly upset.

"What is it honey?" I inquired.

It took every effort within Valentina's disciplined composure to not curse or yell as she slid a piece of paper across my desk.

As she fought to keep her voice at a reasonably low volume, she said, "LOOK… AT… THIS!"

It was a report of new corporations recently filed in the State of New York. Number seven on the list was *MKA Financial, Inc.,* which had three corporate officers.

Michael Kinwell.

Andrei Dimitru.

Kane O'Connor.

Chapter 4
When Two Tribes Go To War

I received a phone call later that day from my office manager Julia. She informed me that Kane set up a new wealth management firm with Andrei behind my back, and the third partner – Michael Kinwell – was the advisor that The Icon and Joseph had turned in to the SEC for insider trading nearly fifteen years ago. This was the guy that I interned *under* when I first went to work for Joseph.

Michael received a five-year sentence back then, but shortly after his release, his parole officer discovered he got involved with some sort of Ponzi scheme, and he ended up back in prison for another 10 years. Michael was just released from prison a second time and contacted Andrei to seek revenge against The Icon and Joseph, but since both of my mentors were now deceased, I became his new target. The next morning, I was on a plane to New York.

Our two tribes went to war.

When I walked into our New York office, it was a ghost town. More than two-thirds of our people were gone.

"Julia, where is everyone?" I asked as she frantically came sprinting up to me.

In a panic-ridden voice, she replied, "Oh my God Vincent! Thank God you're here! I didn't know what to do! Kane has been transferring accounts out to his new firm and he pulled almost our entire Senior Management Team with him! Apparently, he promised all of them equity shares in his new enterprise. Vincent, almost all of our big clients are gone too. I want to kill him Vincent! I literally want to…"

Julia attempted to compose herself, for she was on the brink of erupting in tears. She took this betrayal so personally – almost as much as I did.

"Vincent, that little backstabber poisoned everyone against you practically overnight!" she said.

However in warfare, nothing of this magnitude happens overnight. It takes months and months of planning, scheming, and manipulating people with a web of lies in order to pull something like this off. I was so angry, it felt like there were scorching flames on the side of my face as my blood boiled and my veins bulged out of the side of my neck. I was absolutely furious.

"Kane, that little scumbag! And Andrei! I can't believe this! Why the hell would Andrei do this?" I asked myself.

I immediately called my driver and had him take me to the address listed on their website. On the car ride to their office, I imagined what I was going to say to these traitors. I wanted to rip their heads off and mount them on the walls of my office. As I walked into their office, it looked like a cross between a Silicon Valley start-up and *The Wolf Of Wall Street* movie set. A bunch of millennials sipping on their overpriced pour-over coffees roamed the sales floor, wearing gaudy three-piece suits and fake *Gucci* belts that Andrei probably bought for them on Canal Street. They looked like a bunch of tasteless goons. Most of them were my ex-employees. They all had smug looks on their faces, but none of them had the guts to make eye contact with me.

And there was Kane, pacing in his massive glass corner office with the title CEO on his door. I wanted to walk in there and punch him right in his ugly little face, but before I could do that, Andrei walked up behind me and said, "Vincent, you must leave."

"Andrei! How could you do this?" I asked, knowing I would not get a logical answer.

"It ain't personal Vincent. It's just business. My entire jewelry client list wants to do their investment business with me. So does Kane. He knew you were never gonna make him a boss over there, so I did. He's rollin' with me now, bro. So is Michael," Andrei said in his stern Romanian accent.

I knew this was more than just business. This was definitely personal. Andrei didn't show up at Joseph's funeral service, and although they were never close, we were all part of The Icon's family. He should have shown up out of respect, but ever since The Icon's death, Andrei was different towards me. There had been a quiet distance between Andrei and everyone in our family after The Icon's passing, but I never understood why. We were like brothers back when I first moved to New York, but as time went on, our relationship silently deteriorated. I knew this level of betrayal wasn't just about the money. Andrei had plenty of money. He wanted something else, and it felt like he was specifically plotting against me. I could see it in his eyes as he looked at me with the same disdain one has towards a newly elected President from their opposing political party.

"Look here Vincent, just walk away from New York, bro. You don't belong here, and you don't need any of this. You're rich as hell now that you got everything The Icon left you, plus everything Joseph left you too. You got it all. They didn't leave me nuthin' man. I still gotta hustle for what's mine out here, so just go back to L.A. bro – back to your mommy-in-law's house. Nobody wants you here," Andrei abrasively said, as he stood with his arms crossed.

I aggressively shouted back, "I ain't your *bro*, Andrei... not anymore! And I'm not *leaving* New York either! I'm not letting you steal all of this from me! Hell no!"

Andrei started laughing in his overly confident way that I once found charming, but there was nothing charming about this *new Andrei*. My blood pumped ferociously through my veins like boiling water through a firehose. I would have given anything to wipe that arrogant look off his face.

I turned my back to Andrei and stormed into Kane's office while he was still on a phone call. He looked at me like a little boy who got caught with his hand in the cookie jar. I slowly walked around Kane's office, staring at him the way a great white shark does as it circles its prey before attacking and devouring it.

Kane then abruptly said, "You were never going to make me a partner, Vincent."

"Partner? I made you my Managing Partner at the firm! What the hell are you talking about?" I yelled.

He replied, "Not a *Managing Partner*, Vincent. That's just a title. I mean a *real* partner. An *equity* partner. You were never gonna let me be an owner!"

"First off, you've only been with me for a few years Kane. You think The Icon made me a partner overnight? Or Joseph? Kane, we had to *prove* ourselves to him over and over until he knew he could trust us, and you were on that path!" I exclaimed.

"Well, Andrei told me I'm ready now, and that you've been holding me back. That's why I'm a 30% equity partner and CEO of MKA Financial," Kane boastfully claimed.

Those words came out of an insecure little boy's mouth – one that attempted to overcompensate for his lack of assuredness. Despite Kane's bravado and posturing – chest puffed out with his *CEO* title screaming off his newly printed business cards – I knew this was all a façade. It was *veneer*, just like Michael's fake confidence back when I interned for Joseph.

And there they were, the three stooges.

Michael, fresh out of prison.

Andrei, pumped up with ego.

And Kane, a lost little boy masquerading as a big shot.

Just then, Andrei walked up and wedged himself in between us putting his forehead just inches from mine, and in his threatening Romanian accent said, "Vincent, get outta here and leave Kane alone."

I never felt this level of rage before. I had never been betrayed like this by someone that I invested so much in. I stood toe-to-toe with Andrei, clenching my teeth and clenching my fists.

Andrei then said, "Go back home to Los Angeles… and give Valentina my best. You know I used to give her *my* best every night."

With a cocky smirk on his overly confident face, Andrei then leaned in and whispered in my ear, "Yeah Vincent, you didn't know I used to get with Valentina back in the day, did you? She didn't tell you, huh. Yeah bro, I used to hit that all the time. Tell her *papi chulo* said wassup."

"I'm gonna kill you Andrei!" I aggressively yelled at the top of my lungs, pushing him with an explosive shove.

Andrei stumbled backwards and hit the wall of Kane's office, but I instantly knew I that was a stupid move on my part. Andrei was a big, strong, Eastern European that grew up street fighting with the Romanian mafia before he came to the states, whereas I had never even gotten into a real fight before.

Andrei rebounded off the wall like it was a chain link fence inside an MMA octagon ring, throwing a right cross and smashing my nose followed by a left hook shattering my jaw, dropping me to the ground. Just then, Michael entered the office and kicked me in the face twice, then stomped on my left ear and temple as Andrei delivered a strong kick to my lower back. It all happened so fast.

"Stop! You guys, that's enough! Please!" Kane yelled as loud as he could, pleading with Andrei and Michael.

I could feel the blood gushing out of my nostrils down my lips and chin as I curled up in fetal position. Andrei and Michael stood over me laughing as I was barely conscious.

"Why... why did you guys have to do that? Why did you guys have to... Jesus Andrei!" Kane stuttered as he stood there shaking in disbelief.

"Shut up Kane. Go call 911. Tell them an intruder came into our office and attacked me," Andrei said as he kicked me in my lower back one last time.

"Yeah bro. This was self-defense. You saw it Kane. Vincent assaulted Andrei. In fact, we should press charges," Michael said with a smirk as he fist-bumped Andrei.

In a whisper of a voice, Kane said, "Vincent, are you okay... are you..."

"Kane! 911! Now!" Andrei sternly said.

I must have blacked out because when I regained consciousness, I was being carried out of the office building on a stretcher. Kane must have called 911 just as Andrei had instructed him to, but I was sure Andrei and Michael coordinated their self-defense story as well.

As the ambulance rushed me to the *New York-Presbyterian Lower Manhattan Hospital* emergency room on Gold Street, just south of 14th Street, I couldn't feel my lower body from the waist down and I could barely move my left arm. Once I arrived at the emergency room, they quickly relocated me to a private examination room. I had suffered a concussion, two broken ribs, a fractured ulna in my left forearm, a broken nose and jaw, and a small stress fracture in the L4 lumbar vertebrae in my lower back.

I passed out again in the private room, probably due to a combination of the morphine and embarrassment. When I awoke, Valentina was in the room talking to the doctor about my condition, examining the x-rays. I still remember seeing Cortez sitting in the corner of the room, crying uncontrollably as Isabella tried to console him and calm him down.

"My God honey, look what they did to you. I called the police department and they're on their way to take a statement," Valentina reassured me as she looked upon me with pity.

As I have said many times in my life, nothing emasculates a man more than when he is looked upon with pity, especially by a woman, and even worse, by his own wife.

In my frail state, I whispered, "No. No cops. I'm not filing anything. Just let it go."

"What do you mean? We are definitely filing a police report. They won't get away with this!" Valentina said as tears ran down her beautiful face.

I wearily replied, "No. I'm not going to file anything. Listen to me honey, leave it alone. Please take Cortez home. I don't want him to see me like this. Please."

Valentina agreed that it was better to remove our son from this environment. Just seeing me in my bludgeoned state was too traumatic for any son to see his father in. I was so embarrassed. Andrei had beaten me like I was a damn piñata, making me feel weak and helpless. Plus I knew I couldn't file anything against Andrei because I was the first one to put hands on him, which was such a stupid move. I knew better, but I completely lost my temper after what Andrei said about Valentina. I just wanted to kill him.

This entire experience made me feel like I was less than a man. Having my wife and son see me like this – beaten up because I couldn't defend myself – made me feel inadequate on so many levels. Perhaps it was partially due to the morphine, but in that moment, I just wanted to crawl into a hole and die. I couldn't bear having my family see me like this.

My right eye had a massive gash over it and was practically swollen shut. My jaw was broken in two places and I could barely talk. I was financially beaten down, physically beaten down, and spiritually beaten down by those I trusted the most. I felt like such a fool. The doctor informed me that I would have to stay in the hospital to have some tests run over the next couple of days.

Each day, I would lay in the hospital bed staring at the ceiling, thinking about everything that happened to me. I felt helpless, weak, and pitiful. Tons of bitter thoughts raced through my mind as I compared my relationship with The Icon to Kane's relationship with me. I wanted so badly to replicate that type of Icon-inspired relationship with Kane.

When I first met The Icon, he not only introduced me to his three protégés – Francisco, Joseph, and Andrei – but he also introduced me to his wife, Isabella. He even invited me into his home before I proved myself to him. The way he trusted me from the very beginning was something so special to me, for I had never experienced anything like that before. It was as if he had a level of faith in destiny that surpassed human understanding. The Icon taught me so many lessons about the mentor/mentee relationship and the emotional investment both sides must make in order to create magic together.

I was certainly the beneficiary of The Icon's generosity. The gratitude I had towards this man was something that could never completely be reciprocated. I made every effort humanly possible to work as hard as I could to honor my mentor, but I also made it a point to verbally express my appreciation towards him. I always wanted to make sure that he knew just how much I loved him and how grateful I was towards him. I would often tell The Icon that I would be indebted to him for the rest of eternity, and though he never put that kind of expectation on me, I knew in my heart that I would live the rest of my days on this earth honoring what he had done for me.

When I met Kane, he reminded me of a younger version of myself back when I first met The Icon, and I invested in him the same way The Icon had invested in me. Perhaps that's why I was so heartbroken when he betrayed me. I don't know if I was angrier at him for not being more loyal, or angrier at myself for failing to replicate the Icon/Vincent relationship. It made me question whether I was ever a good mentor at all. Laying in the hospital bed, I just stared at the ceiling all day. My broken arm was immobile, so I couldn't work on my laptop, plus my lower back kept going into spasm each time I attempted to adjust my position in bed. I couldn't make phone calls either because my jaw was wired shut.

Self-loathing guilt tormented my soul as I obsessed over what I could have done differently to prevent all of this from happening. Maybe Andrei poisoned him. I wouldn't doubt it if Andrei was jealous of me. Perhaps he felt like I became The Icon's favorite, and maybe he secretly wished he had my life. Maybe Kane believed Andrei's lies and became a victim of his wicked spell. But what haunted my soul the most was the thought that I was a fraud, and there is no greater blow to a man's ego than realizing that he is not the man he once thought he was. I would go back and forth in my troubled mind, sometimes feeling resentful towards Kane, and sometimes feeling like I had failed as a mentor.

The more I recounted my interactions with Kane over the last five years, I realized that he and the 27-year old version of myself were not as similar as I had thought. When I was first exposed to The Icon's inner circle, I humbled myself to learn from him, and I understood that being the *first* one to trust was imperative. I never worried about The Icon withholding opportunities from me, and I never had a sense of entitlement with him. My goal was to do as Joseph and Francisco had done, working relentlessly within The Icon's kingdom, trusting that one day, I would be able to win over his trust. I never asked him for anything, and as a result, he gave me more than I could have ever imagined.

One of the life lessons I figured out on my own was that *expecting* someone to give you something is the wrong way to live.

Being the first to give and the first to trust certainly puts you in a vulnerable position, but that is the foundation of any great relationship. Joseph and Christine once told me that when two *givers* get together, they can create magic. That's why their marriage was so great. That's also why my relationship with both The Icon and Joseph was so special. We all gave everything we had to each other, with no expectation of receiving anything in return.

Obviously in the beginning, it was a very lopsided exchange of giving, but I did everything within my means to be the first to give. Many times, I would take The Icon and Isabella out for dinner and I would make sure I always picked up the bill. I would excuse myself from the table at the beginning of dinner and pretend to go to the restroom, but instead, I tracked down our server to slide him my credit card, ensuring that I would be the one to pay. Back in those beginning years, I couldn't really afford to do that, but I did it anyway. Both The Icon and Isabella would still scold me for doing this, but I didn't care. I wanted to make sure they knew how much I appreciated everything they did for me.

As I laid in bed recounting the nature of my five-year relationship with Kane, he only paid for dinner once. We must have shared hundreds of dinners together, but he always expected me to pay, even when it was his idea to dine out together. I have seen people reach for their wallet, *offering* to pay when the bill comes, but that is not the same as *making sure* you are the one to pay. It is a fake gesture, attempting to get the social etiquette credit for offering to pay, when in reality, it is just that – a fake gesture. It is indicative of not understanding how to honor a relationship, and with Kane, there were so many red flags I chose to ignore.

I stayed in the hospital for two days, and as much as I detested hospitals, I would have gladly stayed longer if they had let me. Facing my family every day at home in my weakened state was just another reminder that I was in bad shape in every area of my life. But when you take a financial beating as massive as I was getting dealt, there is no time for pity parties. I had to get my butt out of that hospital bed and start trying to salvage what was left of my business.

Chapter 5
Landslide

I was now out for revenge.

My New York office was a fraction of what it once was. We went from forty-seven advisors down to just four. It was literally like starting over from scratch. I was at home in bed for two weeks which gave Andrei and Kane a two-week head start at pillaging my client list in addition to the damage they had already done. My new breakfast was a quadruple espresso, a valium, and a cocktail of opioids. My jaw was wired shut, so I crushed up my pain killers each morning in a molcajete and stirred the finely ground powder into my quad-shot espresso, sipping it through a stainless steel straw. Each time I took a sip, extreme pain shot through my temporomandibular joints where my jawbone connected to my skull. It felt like someone was driving an ice pick into each side of my jaw. The pain killers barely did a damn thing for me.

When I was finally able to get out of bed and leave the house, I wore a cast and a sling on my left arm for the first week and a half. I went from ex-client meeting to ex-client meeting, grimacing and limping the entire way, trying to win them back to my firm. In addition, the constant excruciating pain in my lower back was so great due to my stress-fractured spine, I was popping NSAIDs all day long like they were *Tic Tacs*.

I had a reputation of having an insane work ethic, but it wasn't enough to win back the clients that Kane and Andrei had stolen from me. I placed far too much trust in Kane. The relationships I allowed him to manage were usurped by my ex-protégé. He silently turned them against me, and I knew the battle of undoing the damage of Kane's slander would be a long one.

For the next year, I worked tirelessly, flying back and forth from Los Angeles to New York, trying to rebuild our New York office while still overseeing our Beverly Hills office. I told myself that I would not let The Icon's legacy down. My obsessiveness pushed me to the point where I would stop at nothing to rebuild what was stolen from me and my family, but after an entire year of pushing, I made far less progress than I would have expected, and I started to doubt my own abilities.

At one point, Valentina and I were like silent ships passing each other in the night. I would wake up at 3:30 a.m. and work on my laptop in the living room, then leave for the office at 5:00 a.m. before she woke up. I usually had takeout food delivered to the office for dinner. I worked late, not returning home until 9:00 p.m. or later on most nights. On weekends, I met with potential investment clients for breakfast, and I interviewed new advisor recruits on Saturday afternoons. This was my schedule when I was home on the West Coast. When I was in New York, my calendar was even more jam packed, booked from 7:00am to 11:00pm. I would video conference with Valentina and Cortez every night after my last dinner meeting, usually around midnight Eastern Time, which was only 9:00 p.m. Pacific Time.

I never made time to workout anymore because all I did was work, work, work. My diet also went to hell because I was constantly eating out in restaurants, entertaining business associates, and grabbing food on the go as I hopped from airport to airport. I thought my suits and dress shirts were shrinking until I stepped on the scale for the first time in over a year. I put on a good fifteen pounds. Well, maybe it was twenty. My eyes were constantly bloodshot, my energy was constantly low, and I was more irritable than I had been in a long time. Sometimes Valentina was the undeserving recipient of my frustration. Though I am embarrassed to admit this, I started acting like my father, barking at everyone as they walked on eggshells around me. It was terrible for my business, terrible for my marriage, and also terrible for me as a father. I tried my best to manage my anger and not take it out on my family, but the overwhelming feeling of failure grabbed ahold of my spirit the way drugs grab ahold of an addict's addiction. It was as if I couldn't control my thoughts or feelings. I became a different person – a person I did not like whatsoever. I was desperate for a solution to dig myself out of this predicament, and I didn't know what to do.

I was completely lost.

In order to keep our New York office afloat, our Beverly Hills revenue was subsidizing our East Coast operation and I was burning through money like crazy. After we got raided by Kane and company, our New York operation was left with very little revenue and a huge overhead I had to cover each month. I had employees in that office that were counting on me, believing that I would be able to resurrect the business and restore our success back to the level we had before the betrayal and mass exodus. I made commitments to them that their jobs were safe and that I wouldn't let them down. But after the first year of my resurrection efforts, I had extinguished all our financial resources. The combined cash flow balance of both offices was now running in the red every month, which you can only sustain for a limited time until you run out of money. And that's what happened to me.

I ran out of money.

So I did what every struggling entrepreneur does that has blue skies vision. I took out a business loan. The first $2 million loan only lasted three months, so I took out another loan – $5 million this time. I invested all of it in a new technology platform that I believed would give us the edge we needed to win back clients from MKA Financial – clients they stole from us. But my fintech idea ended up being a massive flop, so I took out another loan – this time an additional $20 million – leveraging 100% of everything I could leverage.

I was all-in.

I hired advisors on salary plus commission instead of commission-only and paid them massive signing bonuses up front in hopes of them bringing over their entire client list. In some cases, that leveraged strategy worked, but with the large majority of them, their optimism ended up writing checks their production couldn't cash.

They were big on promises and short on deliverables.

The Icon would have never used this strategy and neither would have Joseph. The Icon made me struggle financially in the beginning, having me work at *The Hotel 100* to pay my bills while I interned with Joseph at the firm, eating *Top Ramen* for dinner every night. He gave me the tools and the opportunity, but never removed the sweat equity required of me in his meritocracy. He always did things the *right* way, void of any short cuts or band-aids, yet there I was, trying to *buy* my way back into success. I *felt* like a failure because I hadn't recreated my early success after an entire year of practically killing myself, but even worse, I *knew* I was a failure because I tried to take short cuts – something my mentors would have never done, and to make things even worse, I hid all of this from Valentina.

The reason I couldn't let New York go wasn't just because of my ego. It wasn't solely because I made commitments to our employees either. It was because I had leveraged our Beverly Hills operation far beyond reason. I even put up our New York apartment as collateral on one of the loans. Our $5 million apartment was now leveraged to the hilt with two mortgages and zero equity. All of my corporate credit cards were maxed out and I could barely make the interest payments to the bank each month for all the outstanding business loans I had taken. I was now $32 million in debt, hemorrhaging negative cash flow every month, and nobody knew it except for me.

I had put everything at risk.

Meanwhile, I heard rumors that Kane and Andrei's enterprise was growing at hyper-speed. As my empire was crumbling, theirs appeared to be taking off. One night when I was in New York, I saw them at a restaurant on the Upper East Side. There were twelve of them and they acted like a bunch of classless hooligans. Everyone in the restaurant was annoyed with their boisterous table, as Andrei and his cocky big mouth led their obnoxious shenanigans. However the fact that they were all smiling and laughing while I sat there by myself made me feel like they had everything I once had – and it now felt like I had nothing.

The Kane I once knew wasn't loud and obnoxious at all. If anything, he was quiet and reserved just like me, but I suppose money and power revealed the *true Kane*. Kane laughed loudly at all of Andrei's antics, but he seemed uncomfortable in his own skin that night. It didn't matter though. This was the new skin he chose to live in.

I didn't want them to see me, especially because they had their entire team with them, and I was all by myself. I discreetly paid my bill and attempted to sneak out of the restaurant undetected by the MKA mafia, but as I exited the front door, I could hear their table erupt in laughter. I don't know if their laughter was directed at me or not, but I didn't have the guts to turn around and look. I just wanted to get the hell out of that restaurant, especially after the advisor I just wined-and-dined told me he wasn't interested in joining my firm. Seeing Kane and Andrei with their team that night just added insult to injury.

I cringed every time I entered a restaurant, hoping I wouldn't run into Kane or Andrei. It seemed like everything they touched turned into gold, and everything I touched turned into dust. I would go to sleep every night feeling like all of my efforts were in vain.

There were mornings where I would leave the house at 4:00 a.m. for the office, desperately trying to figure out how to dig myself out of this mess. Sometimes – not often – but sometimes, I would just break down and cry. There is nothing worse than having a reputation of being a financial guru, and being in financial ruin at the same time.

I felt myself starting to crack – I mean *really* crack – where I began to feel like I was beyond repair. The hairline cracks in my spirit that I was once able to hide from everyone started to become massive gaping valleys. I had a $50 million life insurance policy on me, and in my darkest moments, I often wondered if Valentina and Cortez would be better off without me. If I died, it would pay off all my debts and still leave my family with $18 million of net cash to replace the failure I had caused. I couldn't believe I was having these thoughts, but this was my dirty little secret I shamefully hid from everyone.

One evening, Valentina, Cortez and I were driving to a restaurant to have dinner, and all of a sudden, it felt like someone had sucked the oxygen out of the air that I fought to inhale into my lungs. It felt like the devil was slowly suffocating me, one breath at a time. Fortunately, Valentina was driving that evening and I was sitting in the passenger seat working on my laptop. If I were driving, I would have surely crashed our car. My fingertips started tingling. Then a numbness gradually began to creep up from my fingers to my palms, from my palms up to my forearms, from my forearms up to my biceps, from my biceps up into my shoulders. Three minutes later, I had lost total feeling and control over my limbs.

"Am I having a stroke right now?" I thought to myself.

Valentina immediately rerouted our drive from the restaurant to the emergency room. She said, "Honey, pull out your phone and..." but I looked at her and shook my head. I literally couldn't move my arms or hands, and surely did not have the dexterity to dial 911. My limbs completely shut down, and I was worried that my internal organs were shutting down too. I didn't want to alarm Cortez in the back seat, but I thought I was going to die on the way to the emergency room that night. I had a sharp pain in the left side of my chest that increased with every breath.

"Is this it? This is how it all ends? In a car with my family watching this whole thing, right after they watched me fail trying to resurrect my business? Really? God, what did I do to deserve this?" my inner monologue said.

Valentina pulled our car up to the front of the emergency room and ran inside to get help. Thirty seconds later, a big burly male nurse ran up to the car with a wheelchair and opened the door.

"Sir, can you get out of the car by yourself?" he asked.

I shook my head and looked at him with a defeated stare. He reached under my armpits and hoisted me up into his arms, placing me in the wheelchair. He rushed me into the emergency room and immediately took my blood pressure and checked my vitals before taking me into a private room.

The doctor ordered an EKG and a blood draw to run a litany of tests to see what was wrong with me. As I laid there in the emergency room bed, I thought to myself, "Well at least I don't have to end my own life now because God is going to do it for me tonight."

I had lost two friends to suicide within the last four years. One was the mother of one of Cortez's classmates. On a family vacation in San Francisco, she left her family in the hotel room one evening, walked up to the rooftop pool deck that overlooked the city, and jumped to her demise. The other was a close friend of mine who had suffered a nasty divorce. One day, his neighbors found him in his backyard – facedown, shot in the head – with an empty bottle of *Jack Daniel's* and a 9mm *Sig Sauer* on the ground next to him.

When people accusatorily label others as *cowards* who have taken their own lives, it absolutely enrages me. These two friends of mine were not cowards at all. They had just reached a point in life where they were so distraught, they felt they could not fix what was broken, and they didn't turn to the right people for help. I couldn't even fathom what a decision like this would do to my family – and I am embarrassed to admit this – but I did think about ending my own life almost every single day during this time.

The compound effect of being embarrassed about being embarrassed is extremely complex. It is nearly impossible to explain this feeling to someone who has never felt this level of despair. It is the feeling of not only letting down those who are counting on you to deliver every day, but also the feeling of being a complete fraud.

Rising to the top and then plummeting to the bottom was a humiliating experience for me, but what was even more humiliating was knowing that my two mentors gifted me their businesses – entrusting me as the custodian of their life's work – yet proving myself unfit. Laying in an emergency room bed for the second time in the last twelve months, I felt deserving of my punishment.

I was in the emergency room that night for a little over five hours as they monitored my heart rate and studied my EKG and blood work. At 11:47 p.m., the doctor walked into my room and said, "Well Mr. Montgomery, the good news is there was no damage to your heart, no blood clots, and no organ damage. Your blood work came back clean. Nothing abnormal. Do you have any history of panic attacks or anything similar to this type of episode?"

"No. I thought I was dying a few hours ago. I feel like a complete idiot now that you're telling me there's nothing medically wrong with me," I ashamedly admitted.

The doctor continued to ask me more questions about what happened in the car ride that evening. He asked me if there was anything stress-inducing that happened in the car – an argument, an email or text I received, or anything out of the ordinary that could have caused an unusual amount of emotional stress. At that point in my life, there was never any one event that was more stressful than another. Twenty-four hours of every day was spent stressing over my fate of guaranteed implosion.

Though the experience in the emergency room that evening was scary, it was far more embarrassing than scary. There was no logical explanation for what happened, and since there was nothing wrong with me medically, I began to wonder if I was completely losing my mind. I also wondered if this was some sort of spiritual attack on me. Nothing made logical sense to me that evening, which just added to my overwhelming feeling of being lost.

Each day I made a conscious effort to talk myself off the ledge and attempt to restore my business. I did everything within my power to rebuild, but my family was suffering an emotional disconnection from me and I didn't know how to navigate these new unchartered waters. My two mentors were no longer here to guide me and give me the perspective I so desperately needed.

I knew I had to come clean with Valentina. I also knew I had to confess my failure to Isabella, for we were living in *her* home. Despite Isabella's noble attempts to make me feel like it was *our* home – and I knew she was sincere in her beliefs about this issue – deep down, I knew it wasn't *my* home, which just further compounded my feelings of being a fraud.

One weekend when I was home on the West Coast, I sat in the living room of the guest house as I did every Sunday morning, sulking and obsessing over my situation. It was about four o'clock in the morning. I stared out the giant living room window into the dark sky above the massive silhouette of my mother-in-law's house. Just then, I heard the front door slowly open, startling me out of my trance. It was Valentina. She gracefully walked in, approaching me in her fluffy cashmere robe and matching slippers.

"Vincent, we need to talk," she said softly.

My body reacted viscerally, tensing up as if I had inhaled freezing cold air from the Antarctic. As I continued to stare out the window avoiding eye contact with Valentina, I let out a long exhale and faintly replied, "What is it?"

"Look at me Vincent," she requested, sitting down on the floor directly in front of me.

"Vincent, why are you doing all of this?" she asked.

"Doing all of what?" I replied in a distant, unengaged murmur. My gaze returned out the window, staring at the enormous main house that was supposedly *ours*, but was definitely not *mine*.

"Honey, look at me. We have plenty of money – more money than we could ever spend. Cortez is getting older, and with your traveling back and forth from coast to coast, you're missing out on being part of his childhood. It's just not worth it anymore. It's making you miserable, and look at what it's doing to our family – to our marriage," Valentina reasoned.

"Well, what do you want me to do? Just give up and quit? I can't do that!" I defensively and sternly said.

Everything about this conversation felt reminiscent of another conversation I had during another stage of my life – a stage that I left far behind me that I would prefer to forget entirely – but here it was again, rearing its ugly head. I said these exact same words to my ex-wife Amber when she told me she wanted to end our marriage. The difference however was that Valentina was no *Amber*. Despite how much of an idiot I acted like during so many phases of our marriage, Valentina always gave me the *white glove* treatment. She slowed the conversation down, de-escalating the intensity, and more importantly, diffused my defensiveness.

"Vincent, of course I'm not asking you to quit. You're not a quitter. You never have been, and you never will be. I love that about you. All I'm saying is that we need to focus on our family life in addition to the business. Vincent, there have been times where I've thought that we should just shut everything down, scale back our lifestyle a little, and just enjoy life. We sold *Madre's Coffee* for $80 million. We still have over $50 million in the bank after taxes," she calmly said.

"No, YOU have $50 million! It's in YOUR trust! And don't get me wrong honey, I think it's amazing what you've done. But that's not MINE! That money is for you and Cortez, NOT me!" I yelled.

"Stop it! Stop it right now, Vincent! There is no *mine* versus *yours*! It's all *ours*! Yes, it's set up in a trust, but we're a team! Everything we have is *ours*! All I'm saying is that we can't keep up this pace. Our marriage is great, but it's starting to suffer due to your travel schedule. And Cortez. Honey, he misses you. He idolizes you, and he's always asking me, *'When's Papa coming home from New York?'* and he doesn't understand," Valentina explained.

"Well do YOU understand?" I accusatorily asked.

I still can't believe I asked her that question. Of course she understood, perhaps even better than I understood. I felt ashamed that I even asked her that question.

Valentina lovingly looked at me, and in an empathetic tone of voice, she said, "Honey. Listen to me. I understand that you're an achiever, and I know what Andrei and Kane did hurt you deeply. You have every right to be angry at them, but don't let their disloyalty ruin what we have here at home. I know you have to go out there and achieve, but you're letting your anger steal joy away from our family."

I knew withholding the truth about the business's financial solvency wasn't fair to Valentina. She had a right to know. I took a deep breath and swallowed heavily several times.

"Valentina, I… uhh…"

I inhaled deeply and exhaled heavily again as a single stream of tears trickled down my left cheek. She gently placed her hands on my face. She could tell there was something greater at stake – something greater than my traveling schedule – and even greater than my financial woes.

"Baby, what's wrong? What's *really* wrong," she asked, kissing me on my right cheek as she wiped the tears off my left cheek.

"Valentina, I uhh… I messed up. I messed up bad. I've been using funds from the Beverly Hills operation to subsidize New York. I've taken out loans. Several loans. Big loans. I even put up our New York apartment as collateral. I'm so underwater right now. I'm thirty-two deep. Million, not thousand," I shamefully admitted.

Valentina smiled and kissed me on the forehead. This was not the response I was expecting.

"Vincent, I already know about all of that," she lovingly stated, as if I just told her I forgot to replace the extra roll of toilet paper in the guest bathroom.

"What? How?" I shockingly asked.

"Babe, I review the financials with Francisco's sister every quarter. She's been our family's CPA ever since I was in college. She's handled the financials for all of my dad's companies. You know that," Valentina said.

"So why haven't you said anything? You knew I was going in debt that much and you weren't concerned?" I dumbfoundedly asked.

"No. Vincent, I never doubt your business decisions. I believe in you, and although this last year has been rough on the business, I know you're getting closer to figuring things out. It's just a matter of time before things turn around," she said.

Most men cannot fathom having a wife that trusts them as much as Valentina trusted me. It made me even more grateful towards Valentina for being the woman she was.

She continued, "Look Vincent, the landscape has changed. This new generation isn't as loyal as we are. They want immediate gratification, and very few are willing to work for it. Of the ones that are willing to work for it, most of them are greedy and want to take shortcuts like Kane. He seemed like a sweet kid, and I know you had big plans for him, but he ended up being like most people – selfish and short-sighted."

"Valentina, I made the mistake of trying to shortcut the system and *buy* advisors instead of grooming them from ground zero the way Joseph did with me – the way your dad did with me. If anyone's guilty of taking shortcuts, it's me," I shamefully admitted again.

Valentina cut me off, saying, "Look honey, I think that was a chance you had to take. Sure it may be different than what you think Joseph would have done, but Joseph never had to deal with anything like this. Maybe he would have done the same thing you tried to do. Who knows? You tried to innovate in the middle of an attack on your business, and maybe it wasn't the right move, but there was no way of knowing that at the time, and you can't beat yourself up for not being able to rebuild the New York office overnight. That just isn't realistic. But I will say this... there's something different this time around. It may seem like I'm not connected to the business, but remember, I grew up watching Papa build his Beverly Hills firm from the ground up. He would teach me what worked and why it worked, which gave me the business acumen to build *Madre's Coffee*. That same intuition he developed within me is now telling me that something in the world has changed since then, and when something changes locally, nationally, or globally, sometimes the business model needs to change as well. The fundamental rules never change, but the way you apply the rules has to evolve, and that's what you're trying to figure out right now – how to evolve."

I swallowed heavily. I had to know something else.

"Valentina. When I was in Kane and Andrei's office, Andrei said something to me... and... I have to ask you something. Did you and Andrei used to date each other before we met?" I sheepishly asked, knowing my question made me look like an insecure schoolboy.

Valentina smiled, not dismissing my question, but looked at me with her compassionate eyes saying, "Honey, I should have told you this back when we were dating, but I just never thought it was a big deal. My father did set me up on a blind date with Andrei when he first started mentoring him. It was just one date... and it was awful. First of all, it was a daytime date – just coffee. Second of all, after the first ten minutes, I was not interested at all. I could tell he was super nervous, and he put up this façade of fake confidence, trying to hide his insecurity. It was such a turn-off. People think Andrei is arrogant, but it really stems from his low self-esteem. He tries to cover it up with all his fake macho-bravado persona, but deep down, he's an insecure little boy who knows he doesn't belong in sophisticated environments. He lacks class and he knows it. Quite frankly, I never understood what my father saw in him."

"But why didn't you ever tell me? Honey, you should have told me," I said in a perturbed tone of voice.

"Vincent, you're right. I should have told you. That was unfair of me. But remember, I didn't know you knew my father until that night at *Amor* when you proposed to me, which meant I didn't know you knew Andrei either. When the big reveal happened that night and I put all the pieces together, we were already engaged. One daytime coffee date with Andrei that happened years ago seemed so insignificant. It was just coffee, but you're right, I should have told you. And I promise you, nothing happened. And Andrei... ewww! He's disgusting!"

As I started putting the pieces of the puzzle together myself, it all began to make sense. Andrei's reaction to our engagement announcement that night was one of shock, not one of joy. And ever since that night, our friendship began to deteriorate, slowly becoming more and more distant.

"Vincent, Andrei was embarrassed that I wasn't interested in him. In fact, I only stayed on that date for about an hour before I cut it short. And the only reason I stayed for that long was out of respect for my father. Apparently Andrei could tell that I wasn't interested, and after that date – if you even want to call it a *date* – he had a meeting with my father. Andrei broke down telling my father that he knew he wasn't good enough for me. I actually felt sorry for him. I think that's why my father tried to help him so much. He took pity on Andrei," Valentina said.

"But nothing happened between you, physically? Andrei said he used to *give you his best every night*. Why would he say that?" I asked, grimacing at what I feared her answer might be.

"Oh my gosh! He said that? Well, I guess I shouldn't be surprised. That sounds like something Andrei would say. Qué mentiroso! What a liar!" Valentina said, laughing out loud.

"So you never had sex with Andrei?" I clarified.

"Vincent, I promise you, nothing like that ever happened with Andrei... or anybody," she said as her countenance completely changed from being light-hearted to extremely serious and sentimental.

Valentina looked into my eyes as she put her arms around my waist, pulling me in close to her and whispered softly, "Vincent, you're the only one I've ever *been* with. I only had a few serious boyfriends before you, and I never had sex with any of them. I was saving myself for the right man, and I know that might sound old fashioned, but that's how I was raised. It's always been you... just you... no one else. Listen to me Vincent, we're going to get through this challenging time together, as a team. No one is going to beat us. No one. Not even the business. But I'm going to ask you something, and you have to be honest with me... and you have to be honest with yourself."

I took another deep breath. Despite anticipating that her question might be a hard one to hear and an even harder one to answer, I nodded my head in acceptance, bracing myself.

"You have to ask yourself if you're doing this for the money, because if you are, we don't need the money. And if you're doing this because you feel guilty that somehow you're letting my father down, you're not. He's been through tough times too when he started *El Cien* back in Nicaragua. If he was here, he'd be in the trenches with you, fighting side by side. He wouldn't be judging you whatsoever. So if you're feeling like that, you have to let it go. And lastly, if you're doing this for revenge, you know darn well that isn't healthy either, especially for you," she said.

"So what's left? If not for the money... or to protect your father's legacy... or for revenge... then for what?" I confusingly asked.

Valentina looked at me with her passionate eyes and said, "THAT is what you need to figure out for yourself. Not for Papa.

Not for Joseph. Not for me or even Cortez. You need to figure that out for you, and you alone. Honey, I will support you in any way you need me to. All I ask is that you make sure you still invest in our marriage, and that you still invest in our son. He needs his Papa, the same way that you needed mine."

Chapter 6

I Need A Doctor

It was months since I last saw Francisco. He had finally retired from his day-to-day responsibilities as CEO and COO of *The Hotel 100* and was finally enjoying a slower-paced life. At least that's what he tried to convince everyone of.

Francisco decided to move into the *Presidential Suite* of *The Hotel 100* as his primary residence. He said it was because he had so many fond memories with The Icon in that suite. I'm sure that was true, but I also knew he couldn't let go of the responsibility he felt as the caretaker of the hotel – The Icon's first major business success in the states. Francisco always took his stewardship role so seriously. It was his way of paying homage to his mentor – his adoptive father – The Icon.

As I walked into the lobby, there was Francisco, coaching the new staff members on how to properly greet the hotel guests with a chilled bottle of water.

So much for *retirement* I guess.

"Mr. Vincent!" he exclaimed, rushing over to give me one of his signature *Francisco* extended hugs.

Most people give a quick cordial hug as to not be too invasive or intimate in a public greeting, but not Francisco. When you received a hug from Francisco, he would hold you close as you felt the love in his heart transfer directly into yours. He would hold you just a few moments longer than what would make most people feel comfortable, but with Francisco, it never felt awkward. Francisco gave this type of hug to everyone. His embrace was often times healing for me, as if he were a doctor and his hugs were the medicine he was obligated to administer. This was one of those occasions. Though my physical injuries were mostly healed, the mental and emotional injuries I suffered through this entire ordeal with Andrei and Kane were still open wounds.

I hugged Francisco a half second longer than he held me this time. He looked at me post-embrace with his hands placed on my shoulders as if he knew I needed some encouragement, but instead of whisking me away to talk privately, he first called over his entire staff to meet me. Well, they weren't really *his* staff, as he was supposedly *retired*.

Francisco inherited the remaining 90% of *The Hotel 100's* equity in addition to the 10% The Icon had already gifted him when he was still alive, and it was clear that being a hands-off absentee owner was never going to be Francisco's style. He always loved being in the trenches. It was his way of honoring everything his mentor had done for him.

"Everybody, come, come, come. I'd like to you all to meet someone very special. I present to you Mr. Vincent Montgomery. Mr. Vincent is one of the most successful people in the investment world. He is a nationally acclaimed author, and he was mentored by *my* mentor, The Icon. Mr. Vincent is very special to this organization, and he started out as a *Hotel 100 Guest Ambassador* just like all of you. He is a legend in this organization because he worked harder than anyone we have ever employed at this hotel. Mr. Vincent, I have a big favor to ask of you. Is there any way you would spend just a few moments sharing with these young people what has made you so successful, especially in the area of communication and customer service?" Francisco asked as if I were some kind of celebrity.

"Listen, guys, I'm nobody special. The *real* special person in the room here is Francisco. He taught me everything I know about customer service. I worked for him for over a year at this hotel and so it's an honor to share with you some of things I've learned from this great man right here," I said, putting my arm around Francisco.

I spent the next hour sharing the many lessons Francisco taught me years ago as they all scrupulously took notes and asked a ton of detailed questions. As I explained the philosophies behind what Francisco taught me – the same philosophies The Icon taught him – I could tell he was beaming with pride, for I retained every single little detail of what he taught me. It was the attention to the details that made Francisco great, and it was his commitment to executing these details to perfection that made him a true ambassador of The Icon's legacy.

After our session, Francisco invited me up to his new permanent residence, *The Presidential Suite*. This was the same suite where I had my second meeting with The Icon, back when I was first extended an opportunity that would change my life forever. Francisco kept it in immaculate condition, not changing one detail of its décor. He was a sentimental soul and felt an obligation to perpetuate The Icon's legacy, even down to preserving the exact aesthetic of this magnificent suite. I sat down on the merlot velvet sofa, as Francisco nestled into the caribou suede chair The Icon used to sit in.

"Mr. Vincent, I ordered lunch for us, but I thought we could chat as we await our Maine lobster salads, if that's okay with you," Francisco graciously suggested.

I proceeded to share with Francisco everything that transpired with Andrei and Kane and the betrayal of my employees, but I didn't tell him about getting beat down by Andrei. My list of embarrassments was infinite, and I certainly didn't need to share my physical injuries in addition to my financial ones.

It hurt Francisco's heart to hear of this news, as he took every attack against our family as a personal attack against himself, for his loyalty to The Icon and everyone in The Icon's inner circle was unparalleled.

"Mr. Vincent, I must be very honest with you. I was never a fan of Andrei. I don't like to talk negatively about people, and I know that Mr. Icon really loved Andrei, but I would often tell Mr. Icon that I feared Andrei would turn against him one day. Andrei never had the same level of loyalty towards Mr. Icon as the rest of us. I always felt that Andrei's loyalty was based on what Mr. Icon could *do* for him, more so than what Mr. Icon stood for. I would share my concerns with Mr. Icon, but he always defended Andrei the way that a father defends his son, even when he knows his son has done wrong. There were several times where Mr. and Mrs. Icon had to do damage control for something that Andrei said or did, and it was embarrassing for them because they would have to apologize to some very important people that Andrei offended. I once escorted Andrei outside one of our events and scolded him for degrading the class that Mr. Icon stood for, and he just laughed it off like it wasn't important. He didn't understand that everything that was important to Mr. Icon became important to me. Mr. Icon did his best to try to *save* Andrei. He would never admit it, but I think he knew that Andrei had major character flaws that could not be repaired. Mr. Icon just refused to give up on him."

Though I admired The Icon's intent and commitment to helping Andrei, I began to resent his misplaced faith in him. Perhaps my resentment came from my own self-hatred and embarrassment of my misplaced faith in Kane. Often times, our anger and criticisms of others are rooted in our own feelings of guilt and self-hatred from investing in people who have betrayed us. It is a feeling of embarrassment and shame – that we have been made fools of – and lacked wisdom and discernment. It makes us feel violated. It makes us feel vulnerable. It makes us feel stupid.

"Mr. Vincent, one of the most valuable lessons Mr. Icon ever taught me was about forgiveness. I know you know *Rule #23: Forgiveness Is For The Forgiver*, but the second layer of that rule is perhaps the most important. We must forgive *ourselves* for making mistakes, whether they be mistakes in poor judgement, or poor decisions, or failing to execute with perfection. None of us are perfect. In fact, in order to reacquaint ourselves with *The Rules*, sometimes we need to fall down – or in some cases, get knocked down. Perhaps this is one of those times for you. I know that if Mr. Icon were here today, he would be incredibly proud of the man you've become. I know this because *I* am proud of the man you have become. I have seen you grow over the years from a young man serving bottles of water in this hotel lobby, to running an entire company, entrusted to you by Mr. Icon himself. That alone is something to be extremely proud of," Francisco reassured me.

The Icon's rules continued to teach me from the grave as his lessons were continually perpetuated through his most loyal mentee – his adopted son – Francisco. It made me realize on an even deeper level that Francisco's duty should be a *shared duty* that I was also partially responsible for perpetuating. Perhaps that was what made me feel like such a failure. I didn't have one shining successful example of a mentee that was still with me, which made me feel ashamed, regardless of how many flattering words Francisco showered upon me.

Francisco then said, "Mr. Vincent, I have someone I want you to meet. I don't know what will come of this introduction, but I have a friend – a relatively new friend – whose insight into your situation may be of value to you. His name is Takeo. Takeo Takashi."

Chapter 7
No New Friends

It was an unusual name – Takeo – pronounced *Tok-eh-oh*. I had never heard a name like that before. With a last name like Takashi, I assumed he was Japanese.

Francisco arranged for me to meet Takeo the following morning in *The Presidential Suite*. On my drive to the meeting, I was on the phone with our New York office, putting out more fires. Valentina called me, but I let it ring to voicemail as I attempted to resolve yet another financial catastrophe. As I walked into the lobby, I checked my voicemail to listen to Valentina's message.

"Honey, I just wanted to wish you good luck on your meeting with Takeo. I know that whatever happens today, you're going to figure everything out, and you're going to build something even greater than anything we've ever done. I love you, I believe in you, and I'll follow you wherever you lead our family. Besos! Besos!" Valentina said in her most enthusiastically positive voice.

As always, her belief in me never faltered.

The greeters recognized me the moment I walked into the lobby, treating me like royalty. One young greeter exclaimed, "Mr. Vincent! Welcome back! Chilled bottle of water, compliments of *The Hotel 100*! Mr. Francisco is expecting you. May I escort you to *The Presidential Suite*?"

"Thank you, I'm good. I can see myself up. What was your name again?" I asked.

"Xavier," the young man replied.

"Okay, thank you Xavier. You're doing a great job by the way. I'm sure you're learning a ton from Francisco. Keep it up," I encouragingly said.

As I walked towards the elevator, I reflected on my early days of working for Francisco and thought about the profound effect he has had on so many young people that worked under his wing. I wondered how many of them truly appreciated these lessons, versus how many of them took them for granted. Statistically speaking, I knew the numbers massively favored hours of life-changing lessons squandered by the masses, and that only a small sliver of the those mentored by Francisco actually made something of themselves. It was mildly depressing on one hand, yet incredibly encouraging on the other hand. I was one of the few that rose to the top by applying every little golden nugget Francisco bestowed upon me. In many ways, that made me feel special despite me plummeting to the bottom.

As I knocked on the door of *The Presidential Suite*, I wondered what might come of this meeting. I obviously trusted Francisco, but I just couldn't imagine what his friend – or anyone – could possibly do to dig me out of this giant hole I was in. Francisco opened the door and as always, he greeted me with a long, warm *Francisco hug*. After his embrace, Francisco ushered me over to the living room where his Japanese friend sat enjoying a hot matcha green tea.

"I'd like to introduce you to my good friend, Mr. Takeo Takashi," Francisco proudly announced.

The Japanese gentleman appeared to be in his late 40's – about the same age as me. He was exquisitely dressed, similar to The Icon, but far more understated. He wore a solid black single-breasted suit with an interesting honeycomb texture, perfectly custom tailored. His slacks had matte pewter side adjusters, eliminating the need for a belt, and had two-inch cuffs at the ankles. His crisp white French Cuff shirt had a discreetly embroidered black *T* placed about four inches above his waistline, just to the left of his black silk grenadine tie. His attire was very simple and elegant. His shoes were simple as well, yet an immense attention to detail was clearly obsessed over. They were handmade, black, whole cut Oxfords – the toes perfectly polished with a finish so mirror-like, the leather looked like black glass. Everything about his style was so subtle that only the most discriminating eye would notice such detail. This was the epitome of understated class.

As Takeo stood up to greet me, he was perhaps the tallest Asian man I had ever met. He stood just over six feet tall and was built like an NFL wide receiver. There was an incredibly powerful energy that radiated from Takeo's spirit, and his mere presence was extremely intimidating. His stoic countenance led you to believe that he reserved the use of his *zygomaticus major* facial muscles to smile only for special occasions. His hair was closely buzzed – the stubble about the same length as his well-groomed five o'clock shadow that accentuated his strong jawline. He had high cheek bones and an intimidating intensity in his eyes.

Takeo had the kind of powerful presence that changed the molecular structure of oxygen when he walked into a room. I didn't know whether to bow or shake his hand. Based on his name, I assumed he was a Japanese National, but I was incorrect as I later learned that Takeo grew up in Long Beach, California. Though he was very passionate about his Japanese ancestry, he was as American as I was. Takeo was *sansei* – a third-generation American citizen – as his grandparents immigrated to the United States in the early 1900's.

I extended my hand to Takeo and he shook it firmly, bowing at the same time – a hybrid-style greeting of East meets West. In a deep voice that sounded like a cross between James Earl Jones and *Optimus Prime*, Takeo said, "It's a pleasure to meet you Vincent. Francisco has told me a lot about you, as well as what you're going through with the mass exodus of your people. I'm really sorry to hear that. I've been through something very similar, and Francisco thought it might be helpful for us to talk. My family and I started coming to *The Hotel 100* a couple years ago, and I've recently gotten to know Francisco quite well, so when he asked me if I'd be willing to chat with you, I saw it as an honor."

Francisco then said, "Gentlemen, I'm going to step away for a bit downstairs. The two of you can stay as long as you like. I hope your conversation is fruitful, so if you'll excuse me, I'll connect with each of you separately later today."

The sound of the massive double doors closing as Francisco exited the suite was like a starting gun, signifying the beginning of our meeting. Part of me felt uncomfortable sharing my woes with a complete stranger, but if Francisco thought it was appropriate, I trusted his discernment. I didn't know how to begin this conversation, but thankfully I didn't have to because Takeo began sharing with me what happened to him in business nearly a decade earlier. It was eerily familiar to what I was going through – almost an exact parallel experience. He had built an uber-successful financial services firm using a similar mentorship-based, aspirational brand as The Icon, but at the height of his success, several of his key people betrayed him as well.

"Vincent, I had young people that I brought into the business right out of college. I mentored them from the ground up, teaching them everything I knew and made them very successful at a very young age. I even stuck with them through several of their personal challenges. I loaned them money. I even had some of them live with me and my wife – in my house – when they fell on hard times, personally. I even had an employee whose wife was going through drug rehab and he took 10 months off to support her. I hired someone to temporarily take care of his clients while he was gone, and all the while, I still kept paying him a six-figure salary. And after everything I did for him, he and a group of some of my other employees got together, started their own firm, and pulled the majority of my firm's clients away with them. Every successful business owner I know has been through something similar. It's just that no one talks about it," Takeo said.

"If that's true, why doesn't anyone talk about it? How come I feel like I'm the only one going through this?" I asked.

"I think it stems from false pride. So many people fear they'll be judged if others find out they've fallen on hard times. They're afraid people will think less of them and spread gossip about them… and quite frankly, they're right. You've heard people say *Oh How The Mighty Have Fallen*, almost in a celebratory kind of way. It's a sad part of the human condition. People have a tendency to constantly compare themselves to others, and so when you succeed, they become jealous of your success, and when you fail, they secretly rejoice in your downfall. I think that's why most people hide their struggles, but I hide my struggles from no one. *Common men* are too embarrassed to admit their failures, so they try to portray a life completely void of losses, but once you've been around the block like we have, you realize there's no such thing as a perfect life. To me, there's nothing more baller than to admit that you've been knocked down and prove that you still have the strength to get back up an soar," Takeo explained.

This conversation was so refreshing to hear. Clearly, I was not happy to hear of this gentleman's past hardships, but it made me feel, well, less of a failure.

"So what happened? What did you do?" I asked.

"I went through a period where I was in a really dark place, and that's when I reconnected with my Japanese roots. After a ton of researching and soul searching, I found out that my family are descendants of *samurai*. You see, the samurai lived by a code of honor encompassing seven core principles. These are known as the seven virtues of the *Bushidō* 武士道 code, and it was this code that brought me back to life. It took me three years to rebuild the revenue they stole from me, but at the end of my fourth year, my business was generating more than nine times the revenue it did at my previous peak. By my fifth year, twenty times. And I did all of this by implementing a completely different business model than what I originally started out with. At that point, I was offered $400 million by a private equity firm to buy me out, and I turned it down," Takeo shared.

My direct nature could no longer be contained. I inquired, "Takeo, I know Francisco asked a favor of you to sit down with me, which I greatly appreciate, but what is it that you're proposing, if anything?"

"I've read your book *The Icon Effect*. Francisco gave me a copy of it last night, and I read it cover to cover in one sitting. It was a fantastic read, and many of the concepts you wrote about in that book I believe in deeply myself. They say empires are never destroyed by the opposing enemy. They're always destroyed from within. That's what happened to me, and it sounds like that's what happened to you too. Sometimes we need some outside perspective to see things clearly, and perhaps that's why Francisco wanted us to meet. I'm offering to teach you my interpretation of the *Bushidō* code. It turned around my business, and Francisco thinks it can turn around yours as well. I only have one requirement," Takeo said, as he stared into my eyes with his intimidating samurai warrior stare.

"What's that?" I asked, expecting him to either charge me massive consulting fees or propose taking an equity position in my firm.

But in his samurai *not-a-hint-of-a-smile* countenance, he simply said, "If this works out for you, you must commit to teaching these seven virtues of the *Bushidō* code to someone in need for no personal or financial gain in return. You must commit to paying it forward."

This was unlike any offer I'd been given before. The Icon, Joseph, and Francisco all mentored me, which I would forever be grateful for, and not to take anything away from their life changing impact on me, but there was a potential reciprocal benefit to them based on my performance. Nothing wrong with that whatsoever, but what made Takeo's offer so unique was that he wanted nothing in return – just a commitment to pay it forward to someone else.

"So what does this entail?" I asked.

Takeo wrapped his teacup in the white linen napkin from Francisco's tea tray. He stood up as he placed it on the floor and stomped on it, smashing it into pieces. He picked up the napkin containing all the shattered pieces and emptied them into a rustic grey suede pouch that looked like it was handcrafted in an obscure Milanese tannery.

"Bring this with you tomorrow night," he said as he handed me the suede pouch along with his business card.

It was a thick matte white card – about three times thicker than normal business card stock. His office was in Orange County, but on the back, there was a handwritten address that read, "*941 East 21st Street, Long Beach – corner of 21st and Martin Luther King Boulevard.*"

"Meet me at this address at 9:00 p.m. tomorrow night, and don't forget to bring the teacup pieces. You're not afraid of driving through *the hood* at night are you?" Takeo asked, again with his stone-faced expression.

"Umm… no, not at all," I replied with hesitant uncertainty.

"Vincent, your business took a massive hit and it isn't what it used to be, but I have a feeling it isn't *supposed to be* what it used to be. When my business was destroyed from within, at first I thought the goal was to restore it back to its previous dominant status, but that wasn't my destiny. My destiny was to build something different – something even greater," Takeo said.

I hesitantly nodded my head in agreement. It sounded good, but when you feel broken and your confidence has been shattered into pieces the way mine was, it's a difficult thing to believe in. Similar to the shattered teacup, my business appeared to be destroyed beyond repair. Even with everything The Icon taught me, and even with my impressive track record of success, I just didn't believe in myself the way I once did.

It was just over a year that I spent attempting to rebuild my New York operation and I had nothing to show for my efforts. My business expenses were still sky-high, and my revenue had not increased much at all. I was drowning financially, falling deeper and deeper into debt, and I had no idea what to do. It felt like I had extinguished all of my creative ideas.

I was completely lost.

It is a difficult thing to articulate – this feeling that you have lost your way with no clear path to redemption. It is enough to destroy a man from within, thought by thought, cell by cell. After going through the betrayal of Kane, I told myself that I would no longer create any new friendships.

No new friends.

However something told me that the universe had sent Takeo to me for a reason. Perhaps my *No New Friends* policy was not what God had in store for my destiny.

Takeo was an extremely powerful man in physical stature, but his aura was even more powerful. In slow motion, Takeo took his index finger and pointed it directly at the middle of my chest. Though he did not make physical contact with me, I felt something very powerful in the energy emitted from the tip of his index finger towards my sternum, and in his deep voice that embodied absolute certainty, he said, "You're in a challenging stage of business right now, but you are *still* Vincent Montgomery. It's time to remind the world who you are – to *reintroduce* yourself. But first, we need to build out *Vincent Montgomery Version 2.0.* "

Chapter 8
Still

That next evening, I exited the 405 freeway on Atlantic Boulevard in Long Beach and headed towards the address that Takeo gave me. I was never afraid of rough neighborhoods, but the closer I got to my destination, the wearier I became. This was definitely not Beverly Hills nor Hays, Kansas – the small town I grew up in. Long Beach was known for its gang violence in this particular neighborhood, and by the looks of some of the characters walking the streets, I knew this was not a safe place for me to be, especially at night.

As I pulled up to the address, I parked my car on the street in front of a small building that looked like an abandoned garage. A chain link fence separated the building from the sidewalk, and there were iron bars on the windows. When you're in a neighborhood where the houses have bars on the windows, you know you're in *the hood*.

I opened the gate on the chain link fence, cautiously walked up to the small building, and knocked on the door. No answer. I knocked again. As I waited, a large intimidating man approached me from across the street. He wore an oversized white t-shirt, baggy black *Dickies* pants with a prominent crease going down the front of each of his pant legs, and black *Nike Cortez* sneakers. His hair was braided in cornrows and he had a menacing look on his face.

"Yo whiteboy, whatchu doin' up in here, cuz?" he asked.

"Umm, I'm supposed to meet someone here," I said.

He could tell I was nervous.

"Oh yeah? Who dat, cuz?" he inquired as he looked me up and down.

I thought for sure he was going to rob me, or beat me up, or steal my car. He just had that *look*. Just then, Takeo opened the door.

"Ay, yo Tok, what up?" the thuggish-looking guy said as he walked over to Takeo.

They exchanged some sort of secret handshake that made me feel like I was even more of an outsider.

"T-Mack, are you giving my friend Vincent here a hard time?" Takeo asked with a semi-smile.

"The white boy's witchu Tick-Tok?" inquired the scary looking guy.

Takeo nodded.

"Ah-ight den. Yo Tok, I get atchu later homeboy."

"You got it," replied Takeo in his deep stoic voice.

Takeo then motioned me to come inside. As I entered the small single-room building, it looked like a cross between a micro-warehouse and an art studio. There were several long wooden worktables positioned in the middle of the room – all of them pretty beaten up – and each table had two chairs on either side, all mismatched. There were several fluorescent light fixtures that hung from the ceilings shining directly onto the tabletops. Industrial-grade aluminum shelving racks lined the walls of the room, each shelf showcasing unusual pieces of pottery. We each took a seat at one of the tables as Takeo handed me a bottle of water.

"Did you bring the teacup pieces?" Takeo asked.

I took the suede pouch out of my jacket pocket and emptied the broken pieces onto the table. He looked at them – each piece – arranging them on the table as if they were pieces of a jigsaw puzzle.

"Are you familiar with the Japanese art of *kintsugi*?" Takeo asked me.

Before I could answer, he continued.

"*Kintsugi* is a process of repairing broken pottery that dates back to the fifteenth century. Ashikaga Yoshimasa – the eighth shogun of the Ashikaga shogunate – once broke his favorite teacup. It seemed beyond repair, impossible to hide the cracks. But one Japanese craftsman made an unconventional decision. Instead of attempting to hide the damage of the cracks, he reassembled the pieces using lacquered resin mixed with powdered gold. The gold actually highlighted the cracks, emphasizing the imperfections, transforming the teacup into a piece of art," Takeo explained as he marveled at the beauty hidden within the broken pieces.

He continued, "You see Vincent, we can learn two of the most important life lessons from *kintsugi*. One, just because something is broken, doesn't mean it should be thrown away."

Before I met The Icon, at times I felt like I was thrown away – discarded by my ex-wife, and at times, discarded by my own father. I knew that level of brokenness very intimately.

Takeo continued, "And two, when we repair a piece of pottery using the *kintsugi* method, our goal is not to *hide* the cracks. Our goal is to draw attention to the cracks – to emphasize and celebrate the cracks – because that's where *the true beauty* is. In life, we're taught to conceal our cracks – our struggles and failures – because society tells us that beauty is about *perfection*, and that perfection *is* beauty. Everything is airbrushed and photoshopped now. You can't even look at a picture on social media that hasn't been edited with some sort of filter. It's the same thing so many people attempt to do with their lives. Everything they show you is *filtered* because they believe that any imperfections, blemishes, or scars take them further away from *beauty*. They don't understand that it's our scars that make us truly beautiful because they tell a story. They remind us that we've been through something – that we've faced adversity – and yet we have *still* survived."

Takeo walked across the room to one of the industrial shelving units and returned with a box containing an epoxy syringe, a small dish, a thin bamboo spatula, and a glass container of gold powder. He emptied some of the gold powder into the small dish and began mixing the epoxy resin and the gold powder together with the bamboo spatula. Piece by piece, Takeo began meticulously reassembling the broken teacup by applying a generous amount of this golden lacquer to each edge of the shattered ceramic pieces. He then pressed the pieces together, holding them until the epoxy began to set. The gold veins that ran along the seams of the shattered pieces highlighted the damage, but as Takeo said, there was a certain beauty to it. As he finished assembling the last piece, the teacup came to life in a completely reimagined aesthetic.

"So what exactly is this place Takeo?" I asked, looking around the room, wondering why such a wealthy man would be sitting in a garage in the middle of the ghetto.

"I grew up here. Well, not *here*, but in Long Beach. I bought this place after I reinvented my company and things started going really well for me financially. My charitable foundation runs an afterschool program here for kids in this community. It's a mentorship-based model where elementary school kids come here after the school day is over, and high school kids help them with their homework, but more importantly, help them navigate through challenges they're facing at home. For the high school kids, it keeps them accountable because they live in the same community as the elementary school kids, so they have to stay out of trouble. They know these little kids look up to them, so they have a responsibility to set a good example. It's kind of a gang prevention program actually. Plus, a lot of these high schoolers are coming from less-than-perfect homes, so they don't know how to open a checking account, and they don't know how to write a resume or apply for a job. So I personally mentor them and help them apply to college, or trade school, or help them get a job. This place is kind of like a little Community Center where we also teach kids how to make pottery using the fine art of *kintsugi*. Every weekend we open it up to the public to sell our pottery, and all the profits go to help fund the charity. We even got *The Long Beach Museum Of Contemporary Art* and the local Police Department to support our efforts. Plus, it gives us the opportunity to teach these high school kids about finances, running a business with overhead expenses, inventory, raw materials, cost of labor and all kinds of things that kids in this community would never otherwise learn from business guys like you and me. I have a little bit of money and some resources, so it'll be interesting to see what this project turns into," Takeo explained.

"So is that why that dude outside was so cool with you, because he knows what you're trying to do here?" I asked.

"Exactly. In fact, T-Mack was an *ICG* member back in the day and got in a lot of trouble when he was a teenager."

"Uh… what's *ICG*?" I asked

"Insane Crip Gang. T-Mack is a *crip*. But he's trying to make a change and make a real difference in this community now. His younger brother was one of our elementary school kids that used to come here to do his homework, and T-Mack used to come pick him up. We got to know each other well, and even though I knew he was gang banging at the time, there was something about him that I believed in. Everyone told me that he was trouble. Drug dealer. Gang member. Violent temper. In and out of *Y.A. – Youth Authority* – that's like prison for underaged kids. But when I sat down with him one-on-one, there was something special about him, and he was always respectful towards me. In fact, he was kind of protective over me. It became a really unique friendship, and as he got older, I stuck with him. Today, he's my right-hand man in our charitable foundation and mentors the high school kids. He's kind of a mentor of mentors now. You see, T-Mack was thrown away by society. He was a broken teacup. But I thought he was worth repairing, just like how we repair pottery using the fine art of *kintsugi*. I taught him that his golden-filled cracks are what makes him beautiful. Perfect imperfection. That's what *kintsugi* is all about. That's what our mission here is all about."

The Icon was involved in several charities and even sat on a few boards of charitable foundations, but Takeo was the architect of this grass roots movement. He was in the trenches with the people. As I looked at this distinguished Japanese gentleman sitting across the table from me talking about his passion for integrating art from his culture into a youth rehabilitation program in this economically depressed neighborhood, I completely forgot about the fact that he was worth over $400 million.

Takeo was dressed in all black. Black jeans. Short sleeve black t-shirt. Unbranded black low top sneakers with black soles. I didn't understand how a man could look so elegant in such simple, casual clothes. There was nothing fancy or expensive about his clothing, yet the way he carried himself with such understated confidence was a modest expression of his true power. His wrist was adorned with an extremely beat-up diver's watch that looked like it had been run over by a thousand cars on the 405 freeway. The *once black* faded bezel was so beat up that some of the numerals had been scratched off completely. Takeo wore it on a black nato strap made of nylon seatbelt material, which unlike his beat up piece-of-junk watch, looked brand new. He saw me taking sneak peeks at his wrist and smiled.

"Are you a *watch guy* Vincent?" Takeo asked.

"Umm, I like watches, but I don't really know much about them. My mentor gave me this one," I said as I pulled up my sleeve showing off my rose gold *IWC*.

"*IWC* makes some nice pieces. That's the *Kurt Klaus DaVinci Limited Edition*, right?" Takeo asked, yet I could tell that he wasn't asking a question. He knew exactly what it was.

Takeo was definitely a watch aficionado, so I didn't understand why he was wearing such a beat-up watch when he was so wealthy.

"That's an interesting watch you have there," I said.

"Are you familiar with *Seiko*?" Takeo asked.

"Sure," I said.

I always thought of *Seiko* as making cheap Japanese watches in mass production, and so I wondered why Takeo would wear something like that. He could afford any watch he wanted.

He explained, "*Seiko* was founded in Japan in 1881 by Kintaro Hattori, a young 22-year old kid that started out repairing clocks. In 1892, he started producing clocks under the brand name *Seikosha*, which means *House Of Exquisite Workmanship* in Japanese, and he eventually created the first Japanese-made wrist watch. He sold them under the brand name *Laurel*, but ten years into his watchmaking journey, his factory caught on fire in an earthquake and burned to the ground and he was forced to start his company over from scratch. Imagine having to start over from ground zero, after all that work he put in. Most people would have given up, but not Kintaro Hattori."

Even with Takeo's watch knowledge and passion for Kintaro Hattori's story, I still didn't understand his choice in wearing this old crusty dive watch.

"This one – the *6105* – is an iconic design. Back in 1979, Martin Sheen wore this same watch in the movie *Apocalypse Now*. Watch nerds nicknamed this model the *Captain Willard* after Sheen's character in the movie. It's such a cool design. The asymmetrical shape of the case. The 1970's styling. The unique integrated crown guard at the 4 o'clock position. This is a very special watch to me," Takeo explained.

"How long have you had it?" I asked.

Takeo smiled again, knowing my question was in regards to the watch's terrible condition.

He explained, "My grandfather was a gardener up in Monterey, California. He was the hardest working man I've ever known. One of his clients was a famous recording artist that owned a mansion in Carmel, and he gave my grandfather this watch as a gift for his 50th birthday. My grandfather wore this watch every day – it was a symbol of his hard work – and when he died, he left this watch to me. People often wonder why I wear such a beat up watch, but it's because they don't understand the backstory of Kintaro Hattori having to start over after his company burned to the ground. They also don't understand my grandfather's backstory – a struggling Japanese-American gardener who never took a day off of work to provide for his family, enduring being locked up in an internment camp during World War II, despite the fact that he was born here. He was a proud American and his love for this country never waivered despite the injustice. He never complained. He never made excuses. He just put his head down and worked as hard as he could, teaching his three daughters to do the same, to honor the family name. His legacy was passed down to me, so I proudly wear this watch every day as he did," Takeo so passionately yet humbly explained.

Takeo taught me that the scratches and imperfections – the *patina* of the watch – contributed towards the beauty of this family heirloom. But it wasn't just the aesthetic qualities of this inanimate object that he admired. It represented a way of understanding life.

81

Though Takeo didn't teach me any directly applicable strategies to employ in my business that evening, perhaps the underlying lessons he taught me were even more important.

By teaching me the art of *kintsugi*, he taught me that even though we may become broken from time to time, we can be repaired – not necessarily restored, but repaired – and that the repaired version of ourselves can be even more beautiful than the perfect and pristine version we so often strive for.

By sharing with me his grandfather's watch, he taught me that the true value of physical objects should not be measured by what someone paid for them, but rather by the stories they tell us – the philosophies they symbolize and the reminders of where we have been and what we have overcome.

By telling me the story of how Kintaro Hattori rebuilt his company after it was burned down to the ground, he gave me hope that I might be able to do the same thing with my company.

Takeo never gave me simple answers to my questions. He used analogies and stories that he knew would resonate with me on a deeper level. The possibilities of what I might learn from Takeo definitely had me intrigued. I just hoped my next meeting with him would be in a neighborhood where I wouldn't have to wear a bullet-proof *Kevlar* vest.

As I drove home that evening, I couldn't wait to share everything I learned with Valentina. This challenging time certainly put a strain on our marriage, but we were unbreakable.

We were titanium.

Chapter 9
Titanium

Valentina and I stayed up all night talking about my conversation with Takeo. She told me that perhaps all of this drama was *supposed* to happen to lead me in a new direction. Valentina always looked at challenges as opportunities and reveled in the uncertainty of the future. She saw every adversity as a launching pad to create greatness, and most importantly, she always believed in me.

I thought about Takeo's explanation of the how the Japanese revered the beauty of the repaired cracks in *kintsugi*, and I was determined to repair the cracks in my life – both in my business, as well as in my marriage. The problem was that I didn't know how to do any of this. I once read a book about the importance of developing your *why*, and I remembered many conversations with The Icon that centered around *my why*. But The Icon also taught me that the *why* is worthless without the *how*. That's what made The Icon, Joseph, and Francisco such great mentors to me. They were meticulous about teaching me the mechanics of *how* to execute, and I hoped Takeo would eventually deliver to me a similar type of playbook.

The following week, I received a phone call from Takeo.

"Vincent, my wife and I would like to have you and your wife over for dinner on Saturday night. Would that work for you?" he inquired.

"Wow, that would be amazing. Let me check with my wife real quick," I said.

After Valentina confirmed our availability that evening, I gladly and graciously accepted Takeo's invitation. I knew nothing about Takeo's wife and I eagerly anticipated meeting her. I found that meeting a man's wife tells you *a lot* about the man, but even more importantly, learning what makes a man's wife tick tells you *everything* you need to know about the man.

Valentina ordered a very impressive floral arrangement to take with us, and I selected a nice bottle of Japanese whiskey – *Old Suntory* – to give to our gracious hosts. As we arrived at Takeo's home in Orange County, it was definitely unique – both the neighborhood and his property. The neighborhood was an equestrian community with sprawling ranch-style single-story homes on massive properties, something not common in Orange County, California. We saw several horse stables on the properties, and even saw one of his neighbors walking her pet bull down the street as if it were as commonplace as walking a dog. Takeo's entire property was surrounded by a tall wall of elephant bamboo – about fifteen feet high. A tall, solid, matte black metal gate was left open for us to freely drive onto the property.

As we stepped out of our car and walked towards the house, we couldn't help but marvel at his incredible estate. There was a large courtyard – about four thousand square feet – that looked like a cross between a desert in Tucson, Arizona and a Japanese Zen rock garden. It brought about a calming feeling as soon as my eyes gazed upon its minimalist qualities. There were several large candelabra cacti strategically planted throughout this clean landscape, with a few palo verde trees and massive rocks strategically placed throughout this landscape as well.

Most of the ground was covered in an arrangement of large asymmetric slabs of oatmeal-colored sandstone, while the ground covering under the cacti and other succulents consisted of pebbles and decomposed gravel. There was an extremely narrow stream – about 24 inches wide – that zigzagged through the Zen garden. An impressive sculpture – a black Brazilian granite arch that stood thirteen feet tall – was placed slightly left-of-center in this courtyard.

As we stood in front of this massive piece of art, marveling at its beauty and unique design, Takeo walked up to greet us. He wore a black long-sleeve Merino wool sweater, black linen pants with a drawstring waist, and black leather Mexican huarache sandals – the authentic kind wherein the soles were made of recycled tire treads. A black onyx beaded necklace hung from his neck with a black tassel that swung just above his waistline.

"I hope the drive down wasn't too bad," Takeo said, extending his hand out to shake mine.

"And this must be the infamous Valentina. I've heard so many wonderful things about you from Francisco," Takeo said, graciously greeting her.

Takeo shook Valentina's hand and kissed her on both cheeks, a very cosmopolitan thing to do – not so *Japanese*, but rather more *European*.

Takeo shared with us that the magnificent sculpture was an homage to a sculpture designed by Isamu Noguchi. Noguchi had a fascination with the massive carved stones you see in his famous rock gardens, writing, *'It is my task to define and make visible the intent of their being.'* The romance of his vision reminded me of the way The Icon used to see people. That's what he saw in me – the intent of my being.

As we made our way into Takeo's home, it was minimalist, yet had no coldness or starkness whatsoever. The walls were done in *siam beige* – kind of a neutral putty color – slightly darker than a vanilla milkshake with a hint of grey undertone. The aesthetic looked similar to Venetian plaster but had a more organic feel with a matte finish – slightly more textured and porous. The corners of the walls were softened with a smooth bullnose finish without a sharp angle in sight. The floors were done in polished concrete and had a marbleized quality to them. A million different tones of grey transitioned from one area to the next, while subtly visible veins ran though the perfectly imperfect concrete slab. These amazing floors had a very *wabi-sabi* aesthetic.

In Japanese philosophy, *wabi* is defined as *"rustic simplicity"* and *sabi* means *"taking pleasure in the imperfect."* Takeo explained to us that this philosophy encourages us to celebrate the way things *are* – the imperfections of life – as opposed to focusing on the way we think things *ought* to be. It is the idea that nothing is really ever finished, but most importantly, it is the acceptance that nothing is ever perfect. According to *wabi-sabi* philosophy, it is the imperfections that we ought to embrace and celebrate, which was very congruent with the art of *kintsugi* that Takeo taught me as well.

Just as I was pondering this concept, Takeo's wife appeared. I don't know why, but I expected her to be… well… Japanese. I envisioned her being a beautiful, yet demure and traditional Japanese woman.

"Vincent. Valentina. I'd like you to meet my wife, Maria," Takeo said.

"Ah! Otra Latina!" Valentina exclaimed.

At least one of my preconceptions was correct. She was indeed beautiful, but she was definitely not Japanese. Her family was originally from a small village outside of Guadalajara in Jalisco. To say that Maria was gorgeous would be the understatement of the year. She wore a traditional Mexican hand-embroidered blouse offset by a pair of fitted distressed jeans and a pair of 4-inch stilettos. On her slender right wrist, she wore a vintage sterling silver cuff with a giant raw chunk of turquoise set in the middle – simple and organic, with understated elegance. I expected to see a giant ice cube sized diamond ring on her left hand, but instead, she wore a simple-yet-interesting silver ring with no stone. Her hair was pulled back and she wore a bun on the top of her head. She wore a pair of vintage filigree silver earrings – very boho-chic with turquoise beads that dangled from the intricate and airy silver frames – handmade by an artisan in Oaxaca. She wore no necklace which accentuated her long slender neck – nothing to detract you from her captivating eyes. Women from the region of Jalisco were known for their beautiful, dark, mysterious eyes.

The two Latinas began an exuberant conversation in Spanish as they marveled at Valentina's floral arrangement, leaving Takeo and I looking at each other with two options.

Option A: Pretend to understand the conversation.

Option B: Grab our Japanese whiskey and take a seat in the living room.

We chose Option B.

Takeo explained to me that Maria's family immigrated to the states from Mexico when she was three years old. Her father was a farmer, and when the Mexican cartel threatened to kill him if he didn't give up his land, he decided to relocate his family to the

United States. Maria's father met an American man that hired him to work in his strawberry fields. He left his family in Mexico to work in California to save up enough money to bring Maria's family across the border. Though they became naturalized U.S. citizens during Ronald Reagan's amnesty program in 1986, they did come here illegally. I know a lot of people have strong opinions about illegal immigration, but if I was in her father's shoes, there's no way I would have stayed in Mexico either. I would have done the exact same thing he did. Her father paid a *coyote* – a man to sneak them across the border – and his family joined him in America for a better life. Maria grew up working in the fields picking strawberries to help support her family when she was only 12-years old. It was difficult to imagine this beautiful, polished woman coming from that type of humble background.

Not only was Maria beautiful and articulate, she was also a master chef – another talent she had in common with Valentina. Adept in multiple culinary disciplines, that evening she presented us with her own unique interpretation of chile rellenos in a wonderful spicy broth, along with a chipotle flank steak garnished with roasted cherry tomatoes. The entire meal was a cultural and culinary experience. The four of us sat at their long oval dining room table. The walnut tabletop was stained black and though its edge was razor thin, it tapered downwards into an upside down cone shape, attaching to a single pedestal base that tapered outwards into the floor, following a similar inverse shape as its table top.

Juxtaposed against the black walnut table were six bleached white oak dining room chairs designed by an iconic Danish furniture designer. The thin, permanently attached seating pads of these sculptural works of art were wrapped in a cream pebble grain leather. Their design was so minimalist, they looked like they would be uncomfortable to sit in, but because of the ergonomic architecture of these masterpieces, they were a treat for any gluteus maximus. Above the table hung a postmodern industrial matte black chandelier. Its bird's nest style arms extended in a multi-directional format and housed seven Edison filament lightbulbs that emitted a warm golden glow.

As we sat at the table enjoying a wonderful dinner, we talked about food. We talked about culture. We talked about art.

We talked about design. Maria wore an interesting ring on her ring finger. When I asked her about it, she became extremely nostalgic.

"Takeo bought me this ring when we were dating, long before his business really took off. The design is in the shape of a bamboo stalk. You see, the Japanese word for bamboo is *take*, pronounced *'tok-eh,'* so the root word of my husband's name is actually *bamboo*. Bamboo is strong, flexible, and nearly impossible to break – just like my husband."

"That is such a cool analogy! I love it!" Valentina exclaimed.

"You know, this ring reminds me why our marriage is so strong," Maria explained as she reached out towards Takeo to hold his hand, gently squeezing it, confirming her love for the strong symbolism of this simple piece of jewelry.

"It's really beautiful. Is it platinum?" I asked.

Takeo laughed, saying, "No, it's sterling silver. Not platinum. Not white gold. Just silver. Nothing fancy. I only paid a couple hundred bucks for it. I was building my first business and I didn't have a lot of money back then."

Maria smiled in an introspective way and said, "That's actually why I like it so much. It's low-key and under the radar. It's funny because a few years after we first got married, my career was peaking, and Takeo's business was really taking off too, so we did what most young people do when they start making money. We spent it. We used to buy so many luxury items. Jewelry. Handbags. Shoes. Exotic cars. It was ridiculous. But a lot has changed since then. We're just not into those types of things anymore."

"You still have beautiful things though. Your home is gorgeous and your art is exquisite. So what exactly changed?" Valentina inquired.

Maria explained, "Sure, we still have nice things, and yes, we do enjoy them. But several years ago, we went through a pretty radical shift in the way we spend money. We realized that a lot of the stuff we were spending our money on was based on trying to create this aspirational brand that we thought was necessary for our business. Our motto was always, *'If we did it, then so can you.'* It all started out with good intentions."

Valentina responded, "Yes! That's what my father always did. But lately, it doesn't seem to work the way it used to. It seems like it only attracts money-hungry people that have no ethics and want a get-rich-quick shortcut to success."

"Exactly," Maria said.

She looked at Takeo, as if she was asking him if she was talking out of turn. Takeo smiled and nodded, confirming that she was an integral part of why we were having dinner together.

"Takeo told me what happened to you guys and how you were betrayed by some of your employees. The same thing happened to us. My husband worked so hard and gave our people so much of himself. He mentored people from nothing and made them very successful, financially. Unfortunately, as their bank accounts grew, so did their greed and their egos. They ended up planning a mass exodus from our firm and stole the bulk of our client base, telling everyone lies about my husband. They even spread rumors that we were going out of business. It was really, really tough," Maria said as she became emotional – her voice slightly cracking as her eyes became glassy.

In an effort to allow Maria to regain her composure, Takeo interjected, "We had a huge overhead, a massive office space, and a ginormous employee payroll. Our revenue got chopped down to practically nothing. We were literally going broke, and no one knew it except for us. I kept going deeper and deeper in debt, tapping every credit line I had to keep the business going. We didn't lay off any of our employees either. I just kept going deeper into debt because I believed I'd be able to turn the ship around and rebuild. But it took a lot longer than I anticipated. I mean, I thought we were going to lose everything."

Maria chimed in saying, "I kept telling Takeo that you can't rebuild a company in two years that took you fifteen years to build. I told him he needed to go all-in with this new business idea he had, and that I didn't care how long it took. I believed in him."

Maria paused for a moment as her voice began to quiver.

"Oh my gosh, I'm so sorry. I don't mean to get all emotional on you," she said, laughing through her tears, fanning her beautiful eyes with the palms of her hands, trying not to let her tears ruin her mascara.

"It's not that those times make me sad. That's not why I get emotional talking about this. It's because I'm so proud of what my husband has created out of those tough times. He says he was afraid we were going to lose everything, but I was never afraid. Even if we did lose everything, I knew we could rebuild our lives and create something even better than what we lost, and that's exactly what Takeo did for our family. Just like *kintsugi*, our life is stronger and more beautiful than it was before it was broken," Maria said, trying to hold back more tears.

Their challenging experience sounded exactly like my situation, and Valentina told me the exact same thing that Maria told Takeo. The difference was that the money Valentina made by taking *Madre's Coffee* public could keep us afloat indefinitely. I never wanted to rely on that, so the pressure I felt – though self-inflicted – was real to me. My company was going broke and I felt like a failure, but Takeo and Maria's situation seemed much more treacherous. They didn't have rich parents or proceeds from another business to fund their challenging time. They had to go all-in at the risk of losing everything they had.

According to Maria, Takeo's second greatest talent was mentoring which came to my surprise because he seemed like such a brilliant mentor, however what she said next made me understand her perspective. She explained that Takeo's greatest talent was *creating*. Takeo had an unbelievable ability to see things that other people could not see – especially voids and opportunities within a market – and his vision of how to create unique solutions was absolutely spectacular. Maria had such admiration for Takeo and she was able to identify and clarify strengths within him that he couldn't identify on his own without her discerning eye. This was one of the many elements that made them such an amazing team.

"Sure, I could have just rebuilt my company using the same business model I used previously. In fact, you could probably argue that it would have been easier to just do that. But I knew it was time for me to create a brand new business model – something completely different than anything I had done before," Takeo said.

"Takeo, were you scared at all about the risk of trying something completely new?" Valentina asked.

Takeo laughed out loud as he leaned back in his chair, saying, "Absolutely! Whenever you're creating something new, you've got about a 99% chance of failure, and that's if you're extremely talented! It took way longer to gain momentum than I thought it would, so we spent the first few years struggling financially, and I mean *really* struggling. There were so many times when I second guessed myself, thinking I made the wrong decision, wondering if I should have just stuck to my original business model."

"Are you serious? I can't imagine you second guessing yourself," I said.

"Oh man, after the first two years of this new business going nowhere, I thought to myself, *'What if this doesn't catch on? What if I end up going so deep into the abyss that I can't find my way out?'* I literally had these conversations with myself every day, reconsidering the fact that I may have made a mistake. This path I took was a risky one because it was intended to completely disrupt a multi-billion dollar industry that was used to doing things a certain way. In retrospect, that was a huge gamble I took," Takeo said.

Maria then argued, "It was never a gamble from my perspective. A *gamble* is when you make a decision that you only halfway believe in. That's the risk of a *gamble*, but when I bet on Takeo, I go all-in 100%. You see, Takeo *believes* in the brilliance of his vision, whereas I *know* his vision is brilliant. There's a big difference between *believing* and *knowing*."

Takeo then jumped in saying, "Even before the betrayal, Maria told me that I needed to ditch the business model of building and multiplying a bunch of *mini-Takeos* and just focus on inventing something completely new. We went into massive debt and I spent the first two years being chastised by most of the industry for my crazy new ideas."

"Takeo, do you ever miss running a big firm with hundreds of employees?" I asked.

He smiled as he shook his head with certainty, saying, "For so long, my identity was wrapped up in being a mentor, and when everyone betrayed me, I found myself being a mentor with no mentees, and a mentor with no mentees is a man with no home – a man with no identity. That really shook me to my core and I went into a very dark place for about a year when all of that happened. I was bitter, angry, and most of all, lost. I literally had to reinvent my entire life's purpose. It was incredibly tough, but it's the best thing that ever happened to me because through it all, it amplified what Maria and I really had – an unbreakable bond with each other. It solidified our belief that we could weather any storm together as a team."

Maria placed her left hand on Takeo's thigh as she stared at her ring finger, saying, "It's like this ring. I *like* the design, but I *love* what it stands for. I love it because my husband gave it to me when we had far less than what we have now. You know, most women out here in Orange County want to walk around flaunting a giant diamond ring on their finger, however I enjoy the irony of doing just the opposite because I don't care about impressing other people with things like that. I'd rather impress them with the quality of my marriage."

Mission accomplished.

I was so impressed with Maria and their marriage relationship. The way she articulated her unpopular stance on her ring selection was something only an extremely confident woman could do. She, like Valentina, had a level of clarity and discernment regarding what things in life are most important. Though they came from very different backgrounds – Valentina growing up in a wealthy family, and Maria growing up with nothing – these two powerful women shared so many things in common. They were both grounded, both driven, and both had an undying love for their husbands.

"What's your favorite gift Maria has ever given you, Takeo?" Valentina asked.

"Our son," Takeo said without hesitation as he kissed her on the cheek.

His love for his family made everything else in life seem almost insignificant, but knowing the context of Valentina's question, he continued, "Maria has given me some very elaborate gifts back when we were big spenders, but my favorite is a recent gift she gave me for my 47th birthday, just one year ago: my 1971 *Ford Bronco*. It's white with a black bikini top on it and it has a few streaks of rust and a long scratch along the driver's side because the original owner drove it through a barbed wire fence. It's loud, the ride is extremely bumpy, it's imperfect, and is void of all modern technology, but it is so fun! Our son named it *El Guapo*."

"Oh that's so cute!" Valentina exclaimed.

"You'll meet him one day, but tonight he's staying at Maria's mom's house. Anyway, of all the cars I've ever had, *El Guapo* is his favorite. I've had some pretty nice exotic cars over the years, but he likes *El Guapo* better than all of them," Takeo explained.

"Why do you think that is?" Valentina asked.

"Because kids don't care about *status*. They only care about the *experience*. Whether you're cruising down PCH in front of the Newport Beach crowd, or you're on a deserted island where no one sees what you're driving, *El Guapo* is fun. That's what's changed regarding how we spend money now. We ask ourselves the simple question, *'Does it make us happier, or does it just stroke our egos?'* and that has fundamentally changed the way we live," said Takeo.

The Icon and Isabella had so many of life's complexities figured out. They built an amazing life together and had an amazing marriage, but Takeo and Maria took it to another level. Rustic luxury, elegant simplicity, and extravagant minimalism was their way of living. It was no better and no worse than The Icon's, but it was different. In many ways, it seemed even more authentic. Though they had the resources to buy virtually anything they wanted, they didn't. For them, it wasn't a matter of practicality or frugality. It was their ability to develop a decision-making matrix to maximize their happiness. To live in such a way where one has so much power, yet exercises such restraint to not show it off was perhaps the most disciplined and authentic way to live.

Takeo also explained that he and Maria only shared their material possessions with those that wouldn't covet what they had. Part of this discipline was rooted in respect for other people's feelings because they never wanted people to feel uncomfortable if they didn't have the material possessions that they had. They believed that bragging and showboating was not only a sign of insecurity, but it was also a sign of disrespect, not taking into consideration the other person's feelings. Takeo and Maria knew that Valentina was still wealthy despite the fact that my business was going broke, so they felt comfortable sharing some of their possessions with us.

"I used to have a collection of over thirty watches. It's kind of embarrassing to admit that I used spend money like that. When we went through that massive business betrayal, we were hemorrhaging so much cash each month, I decided to sell all my watches except for my grandfather's *Seiko*," Takeo said.

"Wow it was THAT bad?" I asked.

"Vincent, you have no idea. Plus at that time, my identity was so wrapped up in my income that when I lost my income, I lost my identity along with it. In retrospect, this reconstruction of my self-image was the most liberating experience for Maria and me."

"How do you mean?" I inquired.

"We started eating at home instead of going out to fancy restaurants, and often times we would cook together as a family, which we never did before. My son absolutely loved helping his mama in the kitchen," Takeo said.

"Cortez loves being in the kitchen with me too!" Valentina exclaimed.

Maria shared, "We also stopped buying all of those unnecessary luxury items. And you know what happened? We realized those things never really made us happy in the first place. Sure we still enjoy nice things, but we realized we used to buy a lot of that stuff for *show*, not for our own personal enjoyment."

Takeo's approach to life was rooted in a set of core principles. This was one of the many things Takeo and The Icon shared in common – their commitment to live under a very specific code of honor, personified in a clearly delineated list of core principles.

For The Icon, it was his *24 Rules*.

For Takeo, it was the *Bushidō* code.

Maria explained that she knew it was hard for Takeo to sell his watch collection when they went through that devasting business betrayal. In fact, she started listing all her jewelry and luxury handbags on an online consignment website because they desperately needed the money to pay their bills. But Takeo wouldn't let her sell any of her things. He only downgraded his own lifestyle and wouldn't allow his financial hardship to affect his wife and son. He always put his family above himself.

Takeo explained that there is a time to cutback expenses when economic hardship hits, but there is also a time to make mindset-oriented decisions that are congruent with where you're *headed*, not where you presently *are*.

Back then, he told Maria, "So what if we go into debt. That's how I started my business. I've been here before. I can do it again, but this time I have more experience, more wisdom, and better resources. We will show no signs of defeat or weakness."

That's what he projected, but he confessed that he didn't actually feel that way inside. He was truly scared – scared to the point where he thought he was going to have a nervous breakdown. I couldn't imagine Takeo feeling like that because he was such a strong force of nature and seemed impervious to self-doubt.

Maria reached over to hold Takeo's hand, saying, "We even took a family vacation to Milan, Italy during all of this, and we paid for everything on airline points and credit cards because we couldn't really afford it – we just didn't have the cash. When we went to the *Bvlgari* boutique on *Via Monte Napoleone*, Takeo wanted to buy me a bracelet for Mother's Day. I told him it wasn't a good time to spend money on superfluous things like this, but he insisted."

"So what did he get you?" Valentina asked.

"There were two bracelets I was looking at, and after I chose one, Takeo secretly pulled the sales associate aside and had her box up both of them. I couldn't believe it. It seemed so extravagant – so unnecessary at the time – but Takeo has always been overly generous with me. Honestly, I don't deserve it... but I must admit, it did make me feel very special," Maria admitted.

Takeo was always like this with Maria because he knew she never expected any of it. In fact, not once in their marriage did she ever ask him for anything extravagant. But Takeo's purchase of those bracelets made a statement to his own subconscious mind, which was, *'We aren't backing down. We will once again be victorious.'* It was symbolic of the faith that Takeo and Maria had in each other, and also symbolic of the faith they had in God. They believed that He would provide the opportunities they needed to create something special during that tough time.

Takeo even sold his diamond-encrusted platinum wedding ring and replaced it with a $10 stainless steel ring he bought from a street vendor on that trip to Milan. Even after his triumphant business recovery, he continued to wear that ring as his one-and-only wedding band. It meant something special to him, making it more precious than any precious metal.

After Takeo's new company began to soar, Maria bought him a very special watch to celebrate the incredible accomplishment of completely reinventing himself, reinventing his business, and successfully rising out of the pit of despair like a phoenix.

As Maria explained her decision to buy her husband this special watch, I looked down at Takeo's wrist, expecting to see a *Rolex Paul Newman Daytona* or a *Patek Philippe Grand Complication* with a minute repeater. Instead, he wore a simple three-hand, time-only watch. It wasn't flashy whatsoever. Takeo was undoubtedly into haute horology, yet he explained that he only owned two watches: his grandfather's old *Seiko* he shared with me at his studio in Long Beach, and the one he wore on his wrist that evening.

"This is a very special watch. The *Credor Eichi II*," Takeo softly yet passionately said, as if he was letting me in on a secret. He removed the watch from his wrist and gently placed it in my hands for me to examine more closely.

"I've never even heard of this brand before," I admitted. I carefully held the watch in my hands as if it were one of only fifty-seven *Fabergé* eggs that existed in the world.

"Not too many people are familiar with the brand. It's actually owned by *Seiko*, and I've already shared with you how I feel about that brand and Kintaro Hattori's story. It's produced in *Seiko's Micro Artist Studio* in Shiojiri, Japan and they only produce twenty of these per year. This watch is very simple aesthetically, but there is so much beauty in its details."

The dial was handmade of porcelain – a painstaking process to create – wherein nine out of every ten shatter during the firing process. Then, an artisan with a very fine brush hand-paints the indices and the logo on the porcelain face of the watch with a tiny little brush. There was only one person in the entire company assigned to this task. When I looked at it under a magnifying glass that Takeo handed me, I noticed that there were even serifs in the font of the logo, all hand-painted. The discipline it must have taken the artist to achieve this outcome was beyond what I could fathom.

Its rose gold case sat on an exquisite alligator strap, dyed in a rich tone reminiscent of an overly ripe blackberry – so dark, it was almost black, but not quite black. The watch was simple and impeccably tasteful, just like Takeo. Its beauty lied in its simplicity and perfect imperfection. The ever-so-slightly variance in the thickness of the hand-painted indices – where each index was slightly raised where the master artist lifted his brush stroke off the white porcelain dial – expressed the *wabi-sabi* element that Takeo and Valentina discussed.

When I asked him how much a watch like this costs, he smiled and said, "It's not about how much it *costs*. It's about what it *symbolizes*. It reminds me of where I came from, what I've been through, and what I stand for."

Maria knew how much Takeo loved Kintaro Hattori's story, and that it felt so similar to what he had to do in rebuilding his own company after it had also been burned to the ground, figuratively. Maria then let out a deep sigh, attempting to maintain her composure. It was clear that she had a deep emotional attachment to that period of their lives together. She snuggled up closer to Takeo, looking into his eyes with so much love and admiration. He was her hero in so many ways, but it was clear that Takeo marveled at her spirit as much as she marveled at his.

Maria had such an exuberant personality which was a stark contrast to Takeo's stoic countenance. She was also very emotionally candid, holding nothing back in sharing how she felt about Takeo, their marriage, and what they had been through, whereas Takeo never showed much emotion at all. He was definitely a *silent samurai* in that regard.

Maria sentimentally shared, "I knew Takeo loved the symbolism and understated nature of this watch. This is the second generation of the original *Credor Eichi*. The *Eichi II* is very similar to its predecessor, but it's larger and simpler, which is symbolic of our lives today: Larger and simpler. Plus, in Japanese, *eichi* means *wisdom* which is also our son's middle name. It was the perfect watch for my husband so I just HAD to get it for him!"

As the evening progressed, I understood why Takeo and Maria's bond was so strong. Though opposite personality types, their permanent bond was solidified by the values they honored together. These virtues were the driving force behind their marriage and how they chose to approach life together as a team.

Once again, that evening with the Takashi's confirmed how important the *right* woman is in a man's life. I've seen so many wives that constantly spend money on unnecessary things in the pursuit of elevating their social status. They also nag their husbands about how much time he spends at work. They complain about everything in their life that isn't perfect, and they care more about how they portray the image of their life as opposed to building a life of real happiness.

At the same time, I've also seen so many husbands neglect their wives. They spend all day Saturday golfing with their buddies, then *Guy's Night Out* on Saturday night, followed up with an entire Sunday of sitting in front of the TV watching sports, and they wonder why their wife nags them all the time.

It works both ways.

In many of the great marriages I've witnessed – The Icon and Isabella, Joseph and Christine, and Takeo and Maria – the one thing they all had in common was that each spouse put their counterpart first, and neither spouse *needed* anything from the other spouse. Each spouse learned how to create their own happiness from within, and due to their self-reliance, they were able to focus on *giving* to their spouse as opposed to *getting*.

As the evening came to an end, Valentina and Maria embraced after exchanging phone numbers. By the energy of their Spanish verbal exchange, I was certain that the two of them would form a long-lasting friendship as well.

On the drive home that evening, I thought about how Takeo's lessons were so esoteric. I remember when he told me we needed to build out *Vincent Montgomery Version 2.0*. Though the idea of recreating myself was exciting, I was sinking deeper and deeper into debt, and I was running out of time. I wanted to just fix my stupid cash flow problems first, and I figured I could always go back later and begin fixing myself, but Takeo was adamant about not rushing the process.

"Fix the business first, and the business will break again. Fix the man first, and the man will become unbreakable. And once *you* become unbreakable, your business will soar," Takeo used to say.

I wanted to believe him. I really did. I just couldn't seem to convince myself that a change would ever come.

But Takeo had different plans for me.

Chapter 10
A Change Is Gonna Come

I woke up the next morning feeling many mixed emotions as I reminisced over my highs and lows, both *with* The Icon, and now *without* The Icon. I walked out to the guest house at 4:23 a.m. and sat down on the patio steps with my Americano. I don't know what came over me, but I started sobbing uncontrollably as I thought about Joseph and how his life was cut short. I wondered if he ever felt the level of despair I felt. I couldn't imagine him ever being distraught, and I certainly couldn't imagine The Icon ever feeling these types of emotions. Even when The Icon was dying of cancer, he never showed signs of defeat despite his impending death. They both seemed impervious to stress, fear, and self-doubt. In many ways, that made me feel even worse about myself.

I was sad, angry, and lost. I missed my mentors. Throughout this entire experience of trying to resurrect my business, I did an incredible amount of deep soul searching, only to come up empty with no answers to my troubled questions. I felt like a shell of a man – empty inside – as if I lost my own soul. When a man has lost his *true north* and feels as though his life is no longer significant, it is only a matter of time before he implodes.

Rancid emotions pumped through my spirit regarding what happened with Andrei and Kane. I had a toxic hate in my heart that burned like battery acid on an open wound. I felt like I was failing my family. I also felt like I was failing my fallen mentors. It is a terrible thing to feel – the feeling of not measuring up to those you love and respect the most. I suppressed my anger and feelings of resentment, burying them deep within my soul to protect Valentina and Cortez from finding out that I was unraveling inside – literally unraveling – as if I were a brand new beautiful sweater with a snag inside that no one else saw, and someone was pulling the thread causing the garment to slowly fall apart.

All of this was undetectable to the outside eye, which was even more destructive to me. When others think you are doing just fine, but you are actually falling apart inside – that is the worst kind of loneliness. When you sink into a place as dark as this, it is easy to lose perspective, and irrational thoughts run wild in your troubled mind causing to you consider the unthinkable.

Perhaps that was what happened to my dear friend Andy. He suffered an awful divorce and his ex-wife did everything she could to poison their two daughters against him. Over time, they grew to resent him. They were young teenagers – thirteen and fifteen years old – and very impressionable. They blamed Andy for everything.

Andy once had a very successful mortgage lending business, but after the crash of 2008, he lost everything. They went from living in a beautiful 7,000 square foot home in Pacific Palisades, to renting a two-bedroom apartment in Reseda. He even had to sell his wife's *S-Class Mercedes* and put her in a five-year old *Toyota Corolla*.

The two met when Andy was already very successful, so she never went through any of the financial struggles Andy went through when he first started his business from ground zero. She had never been *fire-tested*, and unfortunately, he would later find out that she just didn't have the fortitude to stick with him through tough times. His wife and daughters walked out on him a year later.

Andy did everything he could to win them back and mend his relationship with his family for six full years. He never missed an alimony payment, or a child support payment, or any important event that involved his family. In fact, he went into massive debt just to make his alimony and child support payments each month as his business continued to struggle.

Andy never did rebuild his business back to where it was pre-2008, but he was able to build a small boutique firm which was moderately successful – successful enough to buy a new home. Sure, it wasn't a mansion in Pacific Palisades, but it was a cute 1,800 square foot home in West Los Angeles with a small backyard. He bought it hoping that his wife and daughters would one day move back in with him, restoring a modest, downsized version of their previous lifestyle. He couldn't really afford that house, but he had this undying belief that the house would be the catalyst to restore his family. For six years he practically killed himself trying to win back his family, but they had already moved on without him. His ex-wife remarried, his daughters went off to college, and Andy was left alone and depressed. One evening, he decided that without the love of his family, he had nothing to live for.

Andy took his own life in the summer of 2014.

I never understood what could drive a man to the point where he would consider suicide as his only option until now, and although I was not so distraught about my situation that I lost all control of rational thought, I understood firsthand how a man could get to that point where Andy was. Not to disregard what a woman goes through, but for a man, we are taught that our manhood is measured by our ability to financially provide for our family – to *lead* our family – and be regarded as the *Superman* of our household. We aren't afforded the luxury of being depressed, or scared, or sad. I'm guessing that's how Andy felt too.

My heart ached for Andy when he would share with me the angst he felt about his relationship with his daughters. He loved them so much despite their disdain for him. Andy attended one of my motivational speaking events just two months prior to his death and he seemed to be in such good spirits, but obviously that was his way of coping and overcompensating, covering up how he really felt inside.

Rarely is it healthy to compare yourself to other people, however in times of struggle, it is important to remember that there are millions of people in this world that would gladly trade positions with you. Sure, my company was on the brink of financial ruin. Sure, I was betrayed by my employees and my protégé. Sure, I lost my two mentors to premature deaths.

But I had Francisco.

I had Valentina and Cortez.

I had Isabella.

And now I had Takeo.

All things considered, I had incredible people in my life that loved me unconditionally. However similar to fighting in a boxing match, a man can have the greatest people in his corner, but if he doesn't believe in himself, winning is an impossible feat. I had lost all my confidence, my self-worth, and I couldn't afford to pay my bills. The private, dark conversations I had with myself were not healthy ones. When your conscious mind tells your subconscious mind, "I can't win," it is usually the beginning of the end.

In the middle of my self-loathing pity party, I received a text from Takeo saying, "Vincent, I hope it's not too early to text you, but let's meet up tonight. I'll be in L.A. for a dinner meeting tonight that should wrap around 9:00 p.m. Are you available to meet up then?"

"Sure, that's perfect," I texted back.

"Cool. You know where the *Secret Mesa Stairway* is in Santa Monica?"

"Yes."

"Okay, let's meet at the bottom at 9:30 p.m. Wear your gym clothes and bring your running shoes," he instructed.

The *Secret Mesa Stairway* was a 201-step concrete flight of stairs located on the Pacific Palisades side of Santa Monica Canyon. It starts on Mesa Road and rises up to Amalfi Drive, not far from where my friend Andy used to live. It was a workout destination, not as popular as the famed *Santa Monica Stairs* on Entrada Drive where all the aspiring famous and beautiful people did their cardio, but it was definitely a well-known L.A. spot to get a good sweat in.

I navigated through many minefields that day – another exercise in dodging financial bullets and watering dead plants. Practically every attempt I made that day of trying to create fire ended without even a spark as I faced rejection after rejection.

When I arrived at the stairs in Santa Monica that evening to meet Takeo, he was already there. He wore a pair of black gym shorts over black running tights and a black sleeveless workout shirt. He had black running shoes and a stealthy black baseball cap with the words *Takashi Capital* embroidered in black.

As I walked up to Takeo, he extended his hand to shake mine and asked me, "Vincent, how was your day?"

"Good, thanks," I replied.

Takeo continued to grip my hand, and in mid-handshake, pulled me an eighth of an inch closer to him as his eyes squinted at me slightly. Without saying anything, he just stared at me, communicating with his eyes and his grip.

"Actually, today was pretty crappy," I admitted.

I knew that Takeo's grip and extended handshake was about me not being transparent with him. Usually when someone greets you with the common inquiry, *"How was your day?"* it is merely a polite salutation. But with Takeo, he actually wanted to know how my day was. He wanted to know the details – the good, the bad, and the ugly. The special interest he took in people – and in this particular case, me – was part of who Takeo was as a person. As we stood on the sidewalk under the streetlight, we talked for several minutes about how I was doing both mentally and emotionally.

"Vincent, I know you've had to put on a brave face for everyone throughout all of this, as you should. That's what a leader is required to do. If your day was crappy, rarely do you want to share that with people that are counting on you to lead them. But when you're with me, I need 100% transparency. This might be the first relationship you've ever had where you don't need to feel obligated to live up to anything," he said.

He was right. The Icon, Joseph, and Francisco did so much for me, I always felt obligated to live up to an unrealistic self-imposed expectation. I loved and revered them so much, I always wanted to please them and impress them. Don't get me wrong, it was – and is – a beautiful thing. But when you love someone that deeply, there is a small piece of you that holds back just a sliver of transparency because you want them to think of you as highly as you think of them.

As we stood at the bottom of the stairs, Takeo said, "Okay, there are two virtues of the *Bushidō* code I'm going to share with you tonight. The first one is *gi* 義, or *righteousness*. This is the decision to always do what is *right*, especially when nobody's looking, but even more importantly, true righteousness isn't just about what you *do*. It's about what you truly *want* to do – your true intent. Often times, we *say* we want to change, but deep down, we're not ready to do what's necessary. If our true intent is not righteous, it doesn't matter what we *say*. It doesn't even matter what we *do*. In order to embody *gi* 義, our words, actions, and intent must all be one in the same. For example, I used to *say* I wanted to control my temper better, but as I painfully discovered, that was not my true intent," Takeo said.

"So how did you work through that?" I asked.

"I had to admit something to myself that was very hard to admit. The truth was, I didn't want to give up that part of myself. You see, most of the kids I grew up with in Long Beach were either Black or Mexican, so being the only Asian kid on the basketball court, I felt had to create this *tough guy* exterior so I didn't get picked on. I did everything in my power to distance myself from the Asian stereotype of being quiet and passive, so I created this *tough-guy/hot-head* persona, like an Asian version of *Tupac*. That was the emotional shield I created to protect myself from getting picked on, and I carried that emotional shield all the way into adulthood, until I realized that it was stealing joy from my life."

"Wow. What made that shift?" I asked.

Takeo smiled, saying, "When Maria and I first started dating, we were up in Santa Barbara for the day, and this dude looked at me wrong when I was pulling into a parking space. Back then, if someone even *looked* at me wrong, I wanted to fight them. I got out of my car, yelling at this guy, ready to knock him out, and Maria got between us, calmly saying, *'This guy has nothing to lose. You have a business you're building. If you beat him up, you'll get sued. If you kill him, you'll go to prison. He's not worth it, and you're better than that.'* Maria is the only one to ever get me to understand that I was addicted to my anger. I was addicted to my tough-guy persona because it was the mask I hid all of my insecurities behind. Maria helped me understand that I didn't need that emotional crutch anymore – that I was a *man* now, not a *little boy* that needed to protect himself like that. She didn't try to change me. She made me *want* to change, and once that change became something I truly wanted for myself, everything changed."

"So how can I work on my own temper?" I asked.

"The question isn't *how* to change. The question is, *'Do you really want to change?'* Samurai didn't have to *try* to make righteous decisions, and they didn't need an ethics coach to motivate them to do what was right. They actually *wanted* to follow this discipline – even when no one was looking – because it was part of their spirit."

At that time, forgiveness and letting go of my anger was not something that was part of my spirit. I began to embrace the philosophy of *No Good Deed Goes Unpunished*. If my faith in people was a stock, it would have been plummeting at that time. Despite everything I had learned from The Icon about generosity and investing in people, my return on investment felt like I had Bernie Madoff managing my human capital portfolio.

"Vincent, just like you, I also understand through firsthand experience that this righteousness is not always reciprocated. One of the biggest lessons I've learned from my wife Maria is that we cannot allow other people's greediness to make us less generous. We cannot allow other people's lack of ethics make us less honorable. The great samurai warrior Miyamoto Musashi once said, *'Today is the victory over yourself of yesterday; tomorrow is your victory over lesser men.'* This is what *gi* – or righteousness – is all about. Never compare yourself to others. Instead, compare yourself to who you were yesterday, asking yourself *'Am I a more honorable person than I was the day before?'* This is the only thing that matters to samurai," Takeo said.

"But why be generous with people if all they do is stab you in the back? It doesn't seem fair," I mildly argued.

Takeo responded, "True righteousness is the belief in justice as a fundamental. This is the first virtue of the *Bushidō* code, but in order to truly embody this virtue, you must subscribe to the belief that this way of living is what defines you as a man. This commitment to do what is *right* is not something you find among *common men*. Samurai knew they were not *common men* and they accepted the fact that *common men* would often times act dishonorably. They expected this. They accepted this. They embraced this."

Takeo continued, "The second tenet of the *Bushidō* code is *Yū* 勇*,* which translated into English is *courage.* When we go through challenges as severe as what you're going through right now, we have to tap into an even deeper level of courage – the courage to admit that we're lost. You're lost right now, which can be a scary thing to admit, but this is actually the first step in finding the extra gear you need to get through this challenging time."

"Extra gear? Takeo, with all due respect, I'm working as hard as I possibly can right now," I respectfully yet defensively proclaimed.

"Vincent, are you familiar with high intensity interval training workouts known as *Tabata Protocol*?" Takeo asked.

"No, what is that?" I asked.

"*Tabata Protocol* was developed by a Japanese scientist named Dr. Izumi Tabata along with his team from the *National Institute of Fitness and Sports* at Kagoshima Prefecture in Japan during the 1990s. Their research showed that short bursts of high intensity cardio – followed by short recovery periods – conditioned the body much more effectively than longer, monotonous, traditional cardio," Takeo explained.

I had heard of *High Intensity Interval Training* before, but Takeo's explanation of the science behind it was fascinating.

He continued, "*Tabata Protocol* consists of twenty seconds of all-out effort, followed by ten seconds of rest. Twenty on, ten off. Tabata-san's research found that by the second half of this method of exercise, the body was forced to work at maximum capacity from a physiological perspective. This caused the heart to pump faster and the subject's metabolism rate to increase. That's what we're going to do tonight. Let's stretch out first, and then we'll begin."

Takeo took me through a series of yoga-based stretching and breathing exercises followed by jumping jacks – twenty at a time – one jumping jack per second, then ten seconds of rest. Then another twenty-second set of jumping jacks, then ten seconds off.

I thought to myself, "Man, this is easy."

Then twenty push-ups – one push-up per second – then ten seconds to recover. By the end of the second set of twenty push-ups, I was breathing pretty heavily due to the short recovery time of only ten seconds between sets. By the end of the third set of push-ups, my heart was pounding through my chest and I was gasping for air. The lactic acid build up in my pectoral muscles burned from within. Then the climb began.

Forty steps as fast as possible – which took 20 seconds – two steps per second. As he climbed the stair steps with me, Takeo calmly instructed me saying, "Come on Vincent, push yourself harder. You can do it. Show me your *Yū* 勇. Show me your courage."

Takeo always did everything *with* me. It was part of his leadership philosophy. He would always say, "If I do it *with* you, you will run out of excuses as to why you cannot do it too."

The goal of the stairs was to hit two steps per second – forty steps in twenty seconds. Twenty seconds on, ten seconds off. I did the quick math in my head. There were 201 total steps in the *Secret Mesa Stairway*. This would be five 40-step intervals that would put us at the 200th step. I was one interval down with four to go. Takeo was in such incredible cardiovascular shape, he talked to me during the entire climb.

"Each ten second rest should never feel like it's enough to recover. If the recovery time is enough to catch your breath, you're not pushing yourself hard enough," Takeo would calmly explain.

The next twenty-second effort was brutal. My quadriceps burned like hell and my lungs felt like they were going to collapse.

"18, 19, 20. Good Vincent. Now ten seconds of recovery. Relax your mind and your body shall relax. Gain control of your breathing. If you can control your breathing, you can control your thoughts. If you can control your thoughts, you can control your emotions… 8, 9, 10. Let's go again," Takeo calmly stated.

That did not seem like ten seconds of recovery time. I could barely catch my breath. As I began my third of five intervals, my two steps per second turned into one step per second. I stopped to catch my breath, hunching over at the waist with my hands barely hanging onto my kneecaps.

"Come on Vincent. Get your breathing under control. Keep climbing – even if it's slow – for the full twenty seconds. Have the courage to find another gear. Dig deep within yourself to find your *Yū* 勇," Takeo instructed.

I couldn't continue. I stopped, gasping for air, legs trembling. By this time, Takeo knew I was done.

"Okay, catch your breath and once you get it under control, walk the rest of the way up. I'll meet you at the top," Takeo said as he continued his ascension, bouncing up the stairs with the ease of a mountain goat.

I was embarrassed that had I quit. Back when I was in my early twenties, I was in pretty good shape, and even in my 30's, I still managed to get to the gym, but ever since my son Cortez was born, I definitely let myself slip. I had a *dad bod*. I wasn't *fat*, but I was pudgy and soft, and I lost my endurance and overall strength due to my sedentary lifestyle.

Once I got my heartrate down and my breathing under control, I began my *Walk Of Shame* up the stairs. When I finally reached the top, Takeo was shadow boxing under the streetlight. He moved like a young Mike Tyson, bobbing and weaving, throwing super-speed punch combinations. Double left jab, right hook to the body, then right uppercut. He had ferocious hand speed and power, and the foot work of a master. As I walked towards him, he continued throwing his combos and began speaking to me.

"What does it mean to face exhaustion?" he asked, followed by a double left jab as he exhaled twice in synchronicity with his jabs.

"Most of it is in your mind. Slow down your breathing, slow down your mind. Slow down your mind, and you can find your *Yū* 勇 – your true courage," he said, followed by a left-jab-right-cross combo, exhaling with all his might on each punch.

I could tell that Takeo's request for me to join him in this evening's workout had very little to do with the cardiovascular benefits. He wanted to teach me several analogous lessons. Takeo told me that the extra gear required to overcome my challenges was found in these stairs. Takeo said that back when he used to live in Los Angeles, he chose to do his *Tabata* sessions on these steps because there were 201 steps. When he did twenty seconds on, that was forty steps, then ten seconds to recover, then another twenty-second forty-step interval. Five sets of forty steps to get to the top – that was 200 steps to climb, plus one last extra step.

As Takeo wrapped up his shadow boxing, we took a seat next to each other on the curb. He explained the significance of that last 201st step, saying, "That extra step at the top is the difference between being a *champion* and being a *master*. A champion is only great for a *moment*, whereas a master is great for a *lifetime*. Contrary to a champion's goal of being #1, a master seeks out the very best version of himself, which has nothing to do with being #1 because being #1 is about comparing yourself to others. Samurai do not compare themselves to other men. They only compare themselves to the virtues of their code and the man they were yesterday. I remember seeing a champion sprinter in the final 100-meter sprint at the 2008 Beijing Olympics. He won the gold medal and broke the world record with his 9.69 second performance. But watching what was a celebratory feat to most, actually bothered me. I literally couldn't sleep that night as I obsessed over what I saw," Takeo said.

"Why? You just said he was incredible," I asked.

"Incredible talent, yes. Incredible effort, no. When you get a chance, watch the video footage of that race. At the 8.1 second mark, he knew he had already won. He was THAT good. And at that 8.1 second mark, he started showboating and pulled up short. He didn't finish with 100% of his best effort. Yes, he was #1, but that display of showboating made it obvious to me that he was only a *champion*, and not a *master*," Takeo explained.

"But how can you criticize someone who was the best in the world?" I asked again.

Takeo smiled at me like a parent hearing an innocent child say something naïve and explained, "When we're blessed with a particular talent, it is truly a gift. I'm sure he trained very hard, but when a man is given a gift that substantial and chooses to give less than 100% of his very best effort, it's a sign of disrespect to our creator. Now, the very next year, he broke his own record with a time of 9.58 seconds in Berlin – eleven one-hundredths of a second faster. The difference? No showboating."

I could tell this had nothing to do with Takeo's disdain for this world class sprinter as a man, but rather his disdain for a lack of 100% effort in any area of life.

Takeo continued, "On September 12, 2008, there was an article published about a Norwegian physicist at the *Institute of Theoretical Astrophysics* at the *University of Oslo* – who analyzed this 100-meter race at the Beijing Olympics. He and his team of researchers focused on the sprinter's speed, acceleration, positioning, and based on his celebratory showboating twenty meters prior to the end of the race, they calculated that his time would have been somewhere between 9.55 seconds and 9.61 seconds had he not showboated. Now the question is, *'Would his time have beaten his 9.58 world record he established the following year in Berlin?'* We'll never know. Here we are today in the year 2022, and he still holds the world record. But what if someone comes along and runs a 9.57? And what if he could have run a 9.56 in Beijing? Or even a 9.55?"

"You really don't like this athlete, do you," I said.

"I don't dislike him. He's incredible. In fact, I love watching old videos of his races. The way he accelerates is something very special to watch. I just didn't like what I saw in Beijing. It has nothing to do with him personally, but it has everything to do with how *I* want to live *my* life. Comparatively speaking, I have his level of talent in business. Ideas and creativity in business come naturally to me. This is a special gift I'm blessed with, but with great blessings come great responsibilities. My obsessiveness in the areas of effort and extreme discipline is my way of honoring this gift. That's why I say step number 201 is the most important step. 100% effort until the end, plus an extra step beyond what's required. This is the discipline of the samurai warrior," Takeo clarified.

As our workout/philosophy session came to an end, Takeo informed me that it was now time to start digging into the details of my business and developing concrete solutions. As much as I enjoyed these esoteric life lessons that Takeo taught me, I needed to stop the cash bleeding from my company and figure out what my next moves would be. My *why* was obvious, but I needed to discover my new *how*, and I hoped Takeo might be the architect of this much needed rebuild. Takeo told me to come to his office in the city of Irvine the following afternoon for some game planning.

As many losses as I had incurred and as troubled as my spirit was during this time, Takeo told me to look at myself in the mirror every night before I went to bed and audibly say out loud, "I'm still standing." It was an affirmation – my new mantra – intended to remind me that despite how badly I was beaten down, I still had the courage to get back up.

Mirrors are a funny thing. They tell us the truth – a truth that we often do not want to face. I hated looking at myself in the mirror during that time, so much so that I would often avoid making eye contact with my reflection. That's what a man does when he feels ashamed of himself. Takeo told me that I must not only look at my reflection in the mirror, but that I must look at myself in the eyes when I recited my mantra each time. He would constantly tell me that still being able to stand – both literally and figuratively – was something I should be proud of.

That evening, I looked at myself in the mirror right after brushing my teeth and recited those words – *I'm Still Standing* – even though I felt like I was collapsing.

Chapter 11
I'm Still Standing

That next afternoon, I pulled up to Takeo's office building. It wasn't a large building and only four office suites. Takeo's office occupied one of them. The exterior was matte black and looked like something out of a *Mission Impossible* spy movie. Takeo's office was right off the main lobby – Suite 100.

As I entered his suite, it had a similar aesthetic as his home with polished concrete floors, a minimalist warmth, and a *wabi-sabi* feel. It was surprisingly quite small – only about 2,500 square feet – filled with only nine employees. I couldn't believe it. How could Takeo run such a successful operation out of such a small space and with so few employees? I had so many questions to ask him about his business.

I noticed that everyone in his office wore all-black clothing. Some wore black suits, while others wore black slacks and black sweaters. They were all dressed simply, yet elegantly.

His COO came out to greet me. She was an attractive, statuesque Trinidadian woman named Zara. She was in her late 50's, had a charming *Trini* accent, and carried herself with the poise of a *royal*. She wore black linen slacks and a black linen tunic top, and a long strand of polished black obsidian beads was draped around her slender neck. Zara was Takeo's eyes and ears not only with internal operations, but also with his external counterparts.

"Takeo, Vincent is here to see you," Zara said, peeking her head in through the door to his private office.

"Vincent, come on in," Takeo said, walking over to shake my hand and half-bowing as he always did.

I assumed he liked standing better than sitting because he did not have an office desk chair. His desk was more of a large podium on wheels than a desk. It was completely mobile and had just enough desk space to hold his keyboard, mouse, and a notepad. It was positioned directly in front of a wall full of six 42-inch monitors. This unorthodox setup looked like a miniature version of a NASA command center. One monitor displayed his email interface, text messaging interface and calendar; two others displayed incredibly complex spreadsheets, clearly some sort of investment algorithm he was working on; and the three remaining monitors displayed live data feeds of real-time stock market updates.

An asymmetrical sofa was placed against the opposing wall and an Eames lounge chair was strategically placed around a classic mid-century modern coffee table, creating an intimate seating area. Takeo sat in his Eames chair, while I took a seat on the mauve credo asymmetrical sofa.

He smiled as if he knew my every thought saying, "Smaller than you expected?"

I laughed, knowing I didn't have much of a poker face.

"Most people expect me to have a huge extravagant office too. You know, in my old business model, I housed my office in a high rise building over by Fashion Island in Newport Beach. Our facility occupied two entire floors – about 24,000 square feet – and housed over 120 employees. Back then we were doing about $40 million gross revenue. It was a good business... until it wasn't. When all those people betrayed me, I went from $40 million in revenue down to less than $5 million. My basic overhead alone was more than that. Office rent, payroll, tech maintenance, debt service... none of those expenses went away when all of that happened," Takeo said.

I knew exactly what he was talking about. I was in the same exact situation, bleeding cash every month, operating in the *red*.

Takeo continued, "I knew I could rebuild my firm using the same business model that had already made me successful, but I really felt like I had outgrown that model and that I was supposed to create something different – something magnificent. Instead of rebuilding a retail financial services firm going direct-to-consumer as we had always done, I decided I was going to completely shift gears and build a boutique firm that partnered with the top 1% of financial advisory firms in the country. I had this crazy idea of becoming the hired gun that my former competitors would bring in on special assignments to work *with* instead of compete *against*."

"What did they contract you to do?" I asked.

"I built a proprietary software system that could model virtually every single investment strategy a client could conceivably invest in, including hedge funds, index funds, managed portfolios, and of course, my fund. I decided I wanted to build something with real enterprise value instead of just selling a commodity, so I completely repositioned myself from being a competitor of these top advisory firms to being their most valued asset. I partnered with them instead of competing against them, and it completely transformed my business model," Takeo explained.

"Wait a minute, how did you get your former competitors to trust you? Weren't they concerned that you would try to steal their clients?" I asked.

Takeo smiled as if he could read my mind again, saying, "This brings us to the third virtue of the *Bushidō* code: *Jin* 仁. Translated into English, *jin* means *benevolence*. This begins with your true intentions. If your spirit embodies benevolence – to have an authentic inclination to perform kind and charitable acts – the right people will respect you and they'll be grateful for the service you provide. They'll actually *feel* your intentions at the visceral level. I gave so much to my employees for years – just as you have – and to experience that kind of betrayal makes you question everything, but just as Maria shared with you at dinner, we can't let the ill actions of others change who we are. So I built my new business model based on giving these new partnerships access to my secret sauce, and it created a win-win for both parties."

"Takeo, do you think it's possible to be too benevolent? I feel like I gave Kane too much and look what happened. And look what happened to you. You were overly generous with your employees, and they betrayed you the same way my employees betrayed me."

"Vincent, if you believe in generosity, you shouldn't stop being generous. But *discernment* is important too, because if you're a *giver* and you're surrounded by *takers*, the takers will have no boundaries. They'll take from you until you have nothing left – bleeding you dry – with no inclination to reciprocate your generosity. So if you're a *giver*, you can't give to just *anyone*. You've got to partner with the *right* people and give them your very best without holding back. It's like a great marriage. If both parties are all-in with each other, you can build something magnificent together, but BOTH parties must go all-in. That's the only way it works," Takeo explained.

"But how did you get yourself to trust again and go all-in with people after the betrayal?" I asked, knowing I still had trust issues.

"I fully understand what you're asking. I didn't know if I'd ever get over that feeling either, but when I think about my old firm, if my employees didn't betray me, I'd probably still be doing what I was doing back then, and that old business model would have never produced what my new model has. I got an offer from a private equity firm to buy me out last year. $900 million. But I turned them down. I have bigger plans for this enterprise, and I'm just getting started," Takeo said in a calm, matter of fact way.

$900 million. That was just $100 million shy of Takeo's company being a worth a billion dollars. Just a mere 12% increase in his company's value and he would hit that mark. Takeo smiled again, as if he could hear me calculating these numbers in my head.

He said, "The strength of a warrior becomes apparent during difficult times, but a warrior's true strength is demonstrated in times of power. Will we remain respectful and humble when we have an abundance of power, or will we become ego-driven braggarts? This is where *Bushidō* code virtue #4 comes in: *Rei* 礼. In English, *rei* means *respect*. Samurai believed that true respect is demonstrated through maintaining pride and dignity in times of defeat, but more importantly, through humility in times of victory. Common men become boastful in times of victory, treating their opponent with disrespect and gloating over their triumph. I've seen this a lot with people that have become financially successful, especially after they've struggled for so long. They feel the need to show off their success by posting pictures of their possessions on social media, or brag to everyone about the new expensive toy they just bought.

Samurai viewed this type of behavior as disrespectful because it lacks humility. It reveals a person's insecurity, and it shows their need to be validated by others through praise or jealousy. This is what common men do, not samurai."

Takeo already had an incredible amount of power by most people's standards. With all his assets combined, he was already a billionaire, yet his commitment to humility and respect was something that few men could ever exercise. When we had dinner at Takeo and Maria's house, they explained how they exercised *Rei* 礼 by not sharing their possessions with people that have far less than they do. It was an awareness of not triggering other people's materialistic tendencies, for they certainly did not want to inspire covetousness.

To have so much power yet live so modestly was the ultimate display of respect – the fourth virtue of the *Bushidō* code. Takeo was always generous and transparent with me, but he never made me feel like I was accepting charity. He never made me feel like I was less of a man, regardless of how much he gave to me. This was part of his commitment to *Rei* 礼. But in many ways, I felt guilty that he was so generous with me, not because of anything he said or did, but because I knew there was nothing in it for him.

"I have to ask you something Takeo. Why are you doing all of this for me? You don't even know me, yet here you are in the middle of a business day spending time with me. I'm sure you have a zillion other things you could be doing right now," I said as I squirmed uncomfortably in my seat.

He answered, "Francisco asked me to meet with you as a favor to him, and once I met you, I realized this was an opportunity for me to honor *my* mentor. You see, the man that taught me the *Bushidō* code made a deal with me. He told me that the only way I could ever repay him was to teach someone the *Bushidō* code for no personal gain in return. This is the same deal I have with you, right?"

I nodded my head in affirmation, trying to not get emotional. There were seven virtues in the *Bushidō* code that each embodied a stand-alone lesson, yet each virtue was woven together like a beautiful tapestry. They were pure and simple commandments, and

Takeo presented them in a way that made me look at my own life through a different lens, but I had nothing to show for my business resurrection efforts.

"Takeo, I'm so lost right now. I literally have no idea what to do. I've been trying to recreate what I built ten years ago, but it's not working. I promise you, it's not from a lack of effort, that's for damn sure. What would you do if you were in my shoes right now?" I asked.

"That's a tough question. I've been thinking about that quite a bit lately. You're a smart and talented guy. That's obvious. I think the question you have to ask yourself is *'What business model will make you happy?'* If you enjoy your current model, rebuilding what you previously built is not a bad decision. You know how to do it, and you've already done it once, which means you can do it again. But it's possible you may have outgrown that model, and perhaps it's time to transition your old model into something that's more congruent with who you are *today*, and more importantly, who you want to become in the *future*. Let me ask you, prior to those people betraying you, did your business model make you happy?" Takeo asked me.

After thinking through Takeo's question, I took in a deep breath and exhaled uneasily, shaking my head as I embarrassingly admitted, "I thought I was happy, but now I realize it was all a sham. I thought I was perpetuating The Icon's mentorship-based legacy, but look what happened. I'm now a mentor with no mentees – a failed mentor – which means I'm not a mentor at all. And if I'm not a mentor, then I'm nothing."

Just hearing me say that was an audible admission of how I truly felt about myself. There is no lower self-image than being *nothing*. I sunk deeper into my chair, completely deflated.

Takeo then he shared with me a quote: *'All that can be shaken shall be shaken, so that what cannot be shaken may remain.'*

"Where did you get that quote from?" I asked.

"It's actually from the Bible. Hebrews 12:27. This concept can be applied to so many different areas of our lives. The pain you endure from being shaken often times reveals who is really with you, versus who was never with you from the beginning," Takeo said.

"You mean who is *against* you," I clarified, thinking Takeo would emphatically agree with my statement, but I was incorrect in my assumption.

"Vincent, the people that betrayed you aren't *against* you. They're just *for* themselves. They have no honor – no code of ethics – and they don't understand loyalty or character. They're just *common men*. Don't misconstrue their greed and selfishness as a personal attack *against* you. They're just *for* themselves. That's what mere common men do," Takeo explained.

"So who stuck with you?" I asked.

"Some people stuck around for a while, but they thought I was in a weak position because it took so long to reinvent my company. At first, they thought I would bounce back immediately, but it took a few years for me to hit critical mass from a cash flow standpoint. Anyone that understands my true intentions knows that I over-reward people who are loyal to me, and I was building a model that would feed them more opportunities than they could ever create on their own. So I watched how they approached me during this rebuilding process," Takeo said.

"And what did you find?" I asked.

"It was disappointing. These people that I gave so much to – they tried to make me feel like they were doing me a *favor* by sticking with me – implying that *they* were responsible for keeping the lights on. They tried to use that as a bargaining chip to get me to pay them more. During that time, I absolutely hated going to work every day. I distinctly remember sitting in my office, looking out the window one afternoon, and seeing these two guys working on the hardscape of my office building. They were replacing a concrete walkway, and their job was to jackhammer the concrete, break it up into small chunks, and haul it away. The concrete walkway was about six feet wide and about six inches deep with eighteen-inch footers, so this was not an easy job. They were out there in the hot sun all day doing heavy manual labor, and they probably weren't getting paid much to do it. Every day, I would see them working out there, laughing and teasing each other, making jokes all day long. During their lunch break, they would sit down on the ground in the shade and eat their sack lunch, talking and laughing, then return to their work in the blazing hot sun for the rest of the afternoon. It was an awful job, yet these two guys enjoyed their workday because they enjoyed each other, and there I was sitting in a nice air-conditioned office, despising the work I was doing – or more accurately, despising who I was doing it with. Watching those two guys taught me a valuable lesson. It wasn't the type of work they were doing that made them happy, for busting up concrete all day in the hot sun isn't exactly the most enjoyable type of work a man can do. But what made their work enjoyable was *who* they were working *with*. In many ways, I was actually jealous of those guys because I saw the smiles on their faces, and I saw the scowl on mine. That's when I realized I had to create a company that was void of toxic people that dragged my spirit down," Takeo explained.

I could tell this betrayal broke Takeo's heart more than his bank account, just as the people that betrayed me broke mine – especially Kane.

"And so these people lost faith in you?" I asked.

Takeo nodded his head ever so slightly as he walked over to the floor-to-ceiling glass window that looked out onto a small enclosed Japanese Zen garden. He gazed out the window and inhaled deeply, then slowly exhaled at a pace similar to what he used in his *kata* training.

"I really had big plans for them. They just didn't see my vision. I knew I wouldn't need them in my new model, but I was going to bring them along with me for the ride anyway. I was going to set them up for life. All they had to do was honor our agreements, but their greed got the best of them. They just couldn't stop grinding me for more. I finally realized that I was allowing these people to drain me of the energy I needed to successfully create my new venture, and that realization gave me the courage to cut them off and move forward without them," Takeo said.

"Were you nervous about firing those people that were generating the bulk of your revenue?" I asked.

Takeo smiled. He could tell I was dealing with the same issues. Many of my top producing people were trying to grind me for more as well. Some of them even asked me for equity in the firm, which really pissed me off because I could see the hunting nature in their eyes. They saw me as easy prey, not their leader who was financially floating everyone at the firm.

Takeo explained, "Maria and I have this Mexican lime tree in our home orchard. We got it when we first bought our home, fifteen years ago. It was only about waist-high. We kept it in a pot, right outside our kitchen, and it didn't produce any limes for the first six years. Then we planted it in the ground. Again, no limes for another three years. But then it started growing. It shot up to over nine feet tall, seemingly overnight. Building a business is no different. It takes years for the roots to grow strong, and it yields very little fruit in the first several years. Sometimes it takes three years. Sometimes it takes five years. Sometimes it takes over ten, and all the while, you have to water it, fertilize the soil, and feed it. Very few people have the discipline to continue to enthusiastically move forward during this period because you have to put in so much sweaty equity, and you have so little to show for it. The only ones that survive are the ones that have *staying power*. After nine years of struggling, this lime tree started producing the best limes ever. Nine years. I thought to myself, *'Finally, it was all worth it.'* But about a year ago, the tree got a fungus. I was so pissed. I waited nine years, and now it's dying? Maria told me, *'I think we need to prune it all the way back and cut off all the branches with the fungus.'* For the first few weeks, it looked like a dead tree with no leaves and no buds. But after just one week, we started to see new growth coming in, and after four short months, the entire tree had grown back, full in all its glory, fungus-free. I couldn't believe how fast it grew back, and today, it produces even better limes, and more of them. It's just like my business. When I fired all those people, my company looked like a dead tree. I had a big fancy empty office, and it looked like I was going backwards, when in reality, I was pruning my tree, cutting out all the fungus. It took a few years – not a few months – to get things moving in the right direction, but that pruning process was the spark that ignited a fire within me to build what I was *supposed* to build."

Takeo's philosophy of why these people did what they did was the ultimate samurai mindset – the acceptance that these people did not live by any code of ethics just meant they were common men, not *samurai*. They were ducks – not eagles – and you can't expect a duck to act like an eagle. It just isn't in their DNA. Then Takeo shared with me something that Zara told him back when his people betrayed him.

She told him, "Takeo, who you are is NOT a reflection of those that *left you*. Who you are is a reflection of those who *stayed with you* and how we feel about you. We're here because of YOU, and we aren't going anywhere."

Before I was betrayed by my so-called mentees, everyone at my firm followed me like I was the *Pied Piper*. I was running a successful firm, traveling around the country doing book tours and signing autographs at my motivational speaking events. I had people at the firm that looked up to me – so I thought – and I felt like I was really making a difference in their lives as their mentor. I felt like I was picking up the torch that The Icon handed off to me when he passed away. But after everyone turned against me, I realized it was all a ruse, and there is nothing more devastating than realizing that the life you thought you built is nothing more than an illusion.

I felt like such a fraud.

I knew I had to fire some of my employees – the ones that brought a toxic energy to my firm. It would mean an initial loss of revenue – revenue that I desperately needed – but perhaps this pruning was necessary for new growth to occur, and perhaps the new growth would occur faster than I suspected. Perhaps Takeo's lime tree that took nine years to produce its first lime had stronger roots due to its longer gestation period of producing its first lime. Perhaps cutting off all the fungus was the only way for it to heal, and as Takeo mentioned, its healing window of time was far shorter than what he anticipated it would be.

Perhaps my business was that lime tree.

Perhaps I was that lime tree.

As our friendship deepened, there were so many qualities that I admired about Takeo, but the one I valued the most was virtue #5 of the *Bushidō* code: *Makoto* 誠. Translated into English, *makoto* means *honesty*. However the English word *honesty* does not fully encompass the core of what *makoto* meant to a samurai warrior. To samurai, the virtue of *honesty* went far beyond just telling the truth.

Takeo taught me that samurai never used the word *promise* in their vocabulary, and they never had to *give someone their word*. To samurai, *speaking* and *doing* were one and the same, making such distinctions unnecessary. When a common man proclaims to make a *promise* – a distinctly special commitment – it implies that his daily verbal commitments carry less honor. Conversely, for samurai, every word out of their mouths was a reflection of their honor – a reflection of their character. Takeo never *promised* me anything, and he never *gave me his word*, but the level of commitment he had towards rebuilding my spirit went far beyond what any common man could fathom. He embodied each of the *Bushidō* code's virtues, but his commitment to *Makoto* 誠 was something I knew I count on, like the sun rising in the morning.

As our meeting came to a close, Takeo walked me out the front door of his office building, then all the way out to my car, saying, "Vincent, a major shift is about to happen for you, but you have to find that extra gear I've been telling you about."

"But how to I find it? Takeo, I can't work any harder than I already am, I promise you," I ashamedly said as my voice trembled and my bottom lip slightly quivered.

"The extra gear isn't about more *effort*. It's about discovering who you really are and what you're truly capable of. It's about discovering your destiny. You haven't even scratched the surface of what you're truly capable of, but you have to believe in yourself, and right now, I can tell you don't believe in yourself. The lessons embedded in the *Bushidō* code, *kintsugi*, and *wabi-sabi* are the keys to you finding the answers you need, but you have to believe in the principles the way you believe in The Icon's *24 Rules*. We need to unlock your true potential, but it starts with believing that you are more than your past – that you have more inside of you.

Life has knocked you down pretty hard, but you can't let it knock you out. You're greater than that," Takeo said, shaking my hand just before sending me off.

As dark as my situation appeared – and believe me, it was as dark as dark gets – I hoped that Takeo would help me see the light.

Chapter 12
The Light

As I arrived home that evening, I walked into the kitchen to find my family cooking together. Isabella was making *posta sudada*, a traditional Colombian beef dish with tomatoes, potatoes, and cassava, smothered in *aliños* sauce – a delicious savory mixture of peppers, onions, garlic, and cumin.

Cortez was standing next to Isabella, flipping the *arepa santandereanas* – similar to thick tortillas made of yellow corn masa, cassava, and crispy pork belly. He cut one into quadrants on an olive wood cutting board and placed it in front of me on the center island.

"Have one Papa! They're delicious!" he exclaimed.

Cortez loved cooking with Valentina, but even more so with his grandma Isabella. The decision to move into Isabella's home was the right one for so many reasons, but perhaps the greatest blessing was the time my son could spend with his grandma.

Sopa de patacón – a Colombian soup – simmered on the stove under Valentina's watchful eye as she chatted on the phone in Spanish, laughing with exuberance. She smiled at me with excitement as she hung up the phone, running over to give me a kiss.

"I just got off the phone with Takeo's wife, Maria. They're on their way over to have dinner with us right now – her, Takeo and their son Emilio," she exclaimed.

"I just came from Takeo's office and he didn't mention anything about this," I said.

"Oh, just leave it up to the *Latina Connection*. Maria and I set everything up this afternoon. They'll be here at seven o'clock!" Valentina said.

I always enjoyed Valentina's spontaneity. She managed our entire social calendar, and with Takeo's lack of knowledge about these dinner plans, I assumed his wife was the *Chief Operating Officer* of his social calendar as well.

Isabella turned to me and said, "I'm looking forward to meeting these new friends of yours. Valentina told me Takeo is teaching you some new things. It sounds wonderful."

Without saying it, Isabella knew I was in need of either a mentor or a partner, or perhaps both. She was such a big part of my life from the very beginning of my relationship with her husband, The Icon. I still remember the first time she invited me over to their home for dinner – the same home I was now living in. Ever since that day, she has treated me like a son, even before I met Valentina, and long before I officially became a member of her incredible family.

When Takeo and his family arrived and joined us in the kitchen, Maria handed Valentina a beautiful *plum galette* she made for dessert. Takeo handed me a bottle of tequila in an ornate crystal decanter – a bespoke blend of different tequilas he blended himself that even the most discerning tequila aficionados would marvel over. It was a mixture of various blancos, reposados, and añejos that Takeo selected to make his own special blend. Like everything Takeo did, this was something special – something curated by Takeo himself – something that money could not buy.

"This is our son, Emilio," Maria said, gently placing her hand in the middle of his upper-back, introducing him to the rest of our family.

Emilio reached out to shake my hand, looking directly into my eyes saying, "Thank you for inviting us to your home Mr. Montgomery. My father has told me a lot about you."

Emilio was only twelve years old, but he carried himself like a distinguished gentleman. He had a special aura about him as if he embodied the wisdom of an old soul. He definitely lived up to his middle name, *Eichi*. He went around the room, thanking everyone, one by one. This certainly impressed Valentina and Isabella. When he approached our son Cortez, Emilio handed him a book about vintage *Jaguar* cars. During one of my conversations with Takeo,

I mentioned that Cortez loved the design of old *Jaguars*, especially those from the 1960s.

"What a thoughtful gift!" exclaimed Valentina.

"Wow, this is so cool! Thank you so much!" Cortez said, shaking Emilio's hand.

"So what's your favorite *Jaguar*?" Emilio asked Cortez.

"The 1962 E-Type," said Cortez.

"Yeah, that's a cool one!" Emilio confirmed.

The two boys hit it off immediately and headed into Cortez's room. He was excited to show Emilio his pet bearded dragon.

We decided to dine *al fresco* that evening which was Valentina and Isabella's favorite way to entertain. Once dinner was ready, we all stepped outside onto the uncovered section of the patio. Isabella had her long, rustic, teak dining table adorned with a white crocheted center runner and eucalyptus clippings. Tealight candles were strategically placed throughout the table setting that gently illuminated our venue like tiny little stars, and a magnificent arrangement of fresh orange calla lilies was placed in the center of the table that added a wonderful pop of color. As always, the women in our house put on a show-stopping dinner party.

Isabella took a special interest in Emilio.

"So how old are you hoven?" Isabella asked.

"I just turned twelve last month," Emilio said with a relaxed, confident smile.

"Wow, you're so mature and well-spoken for a twelve-year-old... and very handsome too! Tell us what you did for your birthday!" Isabella inquired.

"My parents had a birthday party at our home, and I asked my friends to bring basic supplies so we could donate them to an orphanage in Tijuana that we support... you know, instead of birthday gifts. So they brought things like toilet paper, cleaning supplies, diapers... stuff the kids at the orphanage needed. Plus we raised over $4,000 in donations for them too," Emilio confidently yet humbly explained.

It was amazing to watch this young boy talk about his decision to give up birthday gifts for something he felt was more important. I don't know many common twelve-year-old kids that would be willing to do that, but similar to his parents, Emilio was not *common*.

After dinner, Emilio and Cortez went to play Legos in Cortez's room while the adults enjoyed the amazing *plum galette* that Maria made, along with some rich Colombian espresso.

"I am so impressed with Emilio. He's so articulate for a twelve-year-old," Isabella gushed.

"Thank you. I appreciate you saying that," said Takeo.

"Well, it's definitely a reflection on how you've raised him as parents," Valentina confirmed, nodding to Maria, acknowledging her masterful parenting skills and vision for her family.

Maria smiled back, graciously accepting Valentina's compliment, saying, "Thank you so much. You know, we've really tried to expose him to many different types of people to make him comfortable talking to anyone, regardless of age, race, status… but what's most important to us is that he understands the value and joy of giving."

Takeo added, "When we were going through our challenges in business, Emilio was almost five years old, and I used to have extensive father-and-son talks with him all the time about what we were going through. In fact, every Thursday and Friday night, he and I would sleep in our guest bedroom together. It was our special time to talk about *guy stuff*. In these conversations, I realized it was important for my son to see me struggle from time to time, because if all he saw were the victories, it would've given him the false sense that I was perfect, which I was clearly not. Only allowing him to see the victories would have also sent him the message that he should expect a life with no adversity, which as you know, is not realistic. I wanted him to know that it's okay to go through tough times. The important thing is how he learns to deal with adversity. That's the true test of a man's character."

"You never felt like that was too much to share with such a young child?" asked Valentina.

"Not at all. This younger generation is growing up to believe they're entitled to a perfect life, so when adversity strikes, they're weak. They whine. They have no resilience. If my son never sees me struggle and overcome adversity, how will he ever learn how to work through his own challenges in life? I have to teach him by *example*, not just through words and hypotheticals. During that time when we were really struggling, my son came to me one Thursday evening just as we were getting ready for bed and he handed me $27.32. He knew I was struggling financially, so he emptied out his entire piggy back and said, *'Here papa, this is to help you with your business.'* I couldn't believe this little five-year-old kid was willing to give me everything he had in order to help his dad. It was in his spirit to do this because he was raised in an environment where it was customary to give to those in need, especially to those you love," Takeo said with a warm smile as he reminisced over this tender moment.

"Did you accept it?" I asked.

"You know, on the surface it might seem wrong to accept it, and I certainly didn't have $27 problems at that time. I had $27 million problems. But the joy my son had in his eyes – the pride he had, feeling like he was helping his papa – was something I wasn't going to rob him of. Sometimes the biggest gift of giving is for the giver," Takeo said.

I found it fascinating that Takeo and Maria would put that much faith in their son's maturity to let him experience this at such a young age, but perhaps that was why he was so mature. They didn't let him live in a bubble.

Maria added, "This mindset is based on the sixth virtue of the *Bushidō* code: *Meiyo* 名誉, which means *honor*. We teach our son that honor is the only thing we take with us when we go to heaven, and so Emilio understands the importance of doing the right thing, especially when no one is looking. His identity is rooted in doing the right thing – it's who he is. I always tell him, *'I don't care what the other kids do. You're special. You're a Takashi. That means something.'* So he knows that doing what's right isn't just a reflection on him. It's a reflection on his family's name."

I was not surprised that Maria lived by the same *Bushidō* code as Takeo. She was connected to her husband in a very intimate way and was committed to raising their son in the ways of the samurai. At such a young age, Emilio understood the concept of *honor* in an extremely accelerated way. I asked Maria how she and Takeo taught this concept of *Meiyo/Honor* to their son.

She answered, "Emilio doesn't fear adversity. My husband exposes our son to situations that require making tough decisions, and he talks through his decision-making process with him. He teaches him that if you're a man of honor – if that's who you truly are inside – life will never break you. But it must be authentic. You might be able to hide your dishonorable secrets from the world for a while, but it's impossible to hide from yourself who you truly are."

Maria said something that really resonated with me: *You cannot hide from yourself who you truly are.*

It reminded me of something I used to think about before I met The Icon. Deep down, every man's greatest fear is that one day we might find out who we truly are, and that who we truly are is not who we want to be.

I had spent my entire life hiding.

Even though The Icon molded me into a successful businessman, I found myself hiding again as I faced this new set of adversities. I was so afraid that the success I experienced in business wasn't who I *truly was*, because when everything came crashing down on me, I collapsed like a house of cards. After years of feeling like I had finally *made it*, I now felt like a total fraud. I was still hiding from the insecure little boy I once was – berated by my father, overshadowed by my big brother, abandoned by my ex-wife, and now betrayed by my employees. It seemed that even Emilio at the tender age of five already mastered *Bushidō* virtue #6: *Meiyo/Honor*. He honored his father, giving him the only $27.32

he had, having complete faith in who his father was, what he was capable of overcoming, and what he would eventually manifest. This is who Emilio *truly* was – confident and authentic. It was part of his spirit.

Seven years later at the age of twelve, he was confident enough to forego birthday gifts so that kids at an orphanage in Mexico could have basic things like toilet paper. Emilio had certainty in his heart that this was the proper way to live. I on the other hand was a full-grown adult, yet I was lost again with no confidence and no certainty whatsoever. It was an embarrassing thing to admit.

After our guests left for the evening and Cortez went to bed, Isabella and Valentina sat by the pool talking as I cleaned up the kitchen. They were clearly having a deep conversation.

"Mama, I don't understand why Vincent is killing himself to rebuild everything. We have enough money to do whatever we want now, but he's putting so much pressure on himself to seek revenge on Kane and Andrei. It's not healthy," Valentina discreetly shared with her mother.

"Aye, Valentina. You know Vincent is a man of honor, just like your father was. Papa would have done the same thing Vincent is trying to do right now. Papa never shared with you what happened with *his* business partner," Isabella said.

"Partner? Papa never had a partner," Valentina assumed.

"Oh honey, Papa hid his struggles from everyone except me. He made me swear to never share our hard times with anyone. He never wanted to burden anyone with his problems, but he had terrible problems with a partner in his early days of building *The Hotel 100.* Her name was Joan Gastineau. I never liked that woman. She made Papa all kinds of promises that she had all the right connections in Beverly Hills, so he gave her equity in the hotel. Joan made a lot of announcements, but never really produced anything of real value. One day, Papa overheard her talking disrespectfully to Francisco, using racial slurs and saying all kinds of demeaning things towards him, so Papa decided to buy out Joan's shares in the hotel – grossly overpaying for them – just to get rid of her. The very next week, Joan went around town telling everyone how Papa had screwed her out of millions of dollars. Joan even filed a ridiculous lawsuit against us, claiming we did all kinds of nonsensical things. Hostile work environment. Sexual harassment. You name it."

"So what happened?" Valentina asked.

"Well, Joan came from a wealthy family here in Beverly Hills, so she used her family's money and influence to try to ruin Papa's reputation. At first, a lot of important people believed her because she spread rumors about us to everyone. *Chismosa*! But over time, people realized that Papa was a good man, and that she was a manipulative and deceitful *bruja*. Sure Papa's reputation was questioned at first, and it did hurt the business temporarily. Between the lawsuit and the damage it did to *The Hotel 100's* reputation, we were in a challenging position, financially. This was all before we were even married," Isabella shared.

"Aye dios mio! So what did you do?" Valentina inquired.

"Papa had to practically beg for meetings with everyone that Joan turned against him. He was taking people out to dinner every night, attempting to repair these important relationships. He didn't even let Francisco know what was going on. He was living in this giant house with a huge mortgage, a huge overhead with kids to take care of, and he was afraid he was going to lose everything. On several occasions, he wanted me to come with him to these dinner meetings where he invited both the husband and the wife. He said I was his *secret weapon*. He told me that the most valuable conversation was not the one we had at the dinner table – rather it was the one in the car ride home between the husband and the wife. If I could win over the wife, the wife would tell her husband that we were good people to partner with. But during that time, he was living off credit, going deeper and deeper into debt," Isabella explained.

"So what ever happened to that *bruja* Joan?" Valentina inquired.

"Joan was trying to get Papa to settle, but he never gave in. The case went all the way to trial, and after the jury heard testimonies from all the witnesses, they found Papa innocent. So he counter-sued Joan for defamation of character and torturous business interference, and he won a $15 million settlement. That's what brought him back to life, financially. Your father has always been a master at turning lemons into lemonade," Isabella proudly stated.

"I don't understand why didn't Papa share any of this with me! Why didn't he ever tell me about any of this?"

"That was his way. He never talked about his hardships with people. He didn't want anyone to feel sorry for him," Isabella explained.

"But what does any of this have to do with Vincent? Papa had to recover financially in order to pay his bills, so I understand why he was so obsessed with rebuilding. But for me and Vincent, we have so much left over from the *Madre's Coffee* I.P.O., we don't *need* the money!" Valentina exclaimed.

"Honey, I think you're missing the point. You may not *need* the money, but your husband *needs* to restore his honor. Vincent is a man of honor, just like Papa was. You need to support him. You need to encourage him. It'll be tough on you, and it'll be tough on all of us living under this roof, but our family needs to stick together. Can't you see it on Vincent's face? He's living in a $60 million house he didn't buy himself. He's living off the money you made when you took *Madre's Coffee* public. His business is under attack and his company is buried in debt. Vincent is an honorable man, and I can tell he needs to dig himself out of this mess to restore his manhood. I think this new relationship with Takeo might be just what he needs. He's lost his two mentors, and now he's facing this battle all on his own. We need to support him, now more than ever," Isabella said.

"But what about Cortez? What about spending time with our family? We're in a situation now where Vincent doesn't even need to work anymore. Isn't raising our son more important than rebuilding his company? I'm afraid that if this battle continues for the next five to ten years, Vincent is going to miss out on Cortez's childhood, and Cortez is going to miss out on having his father by his side. We can't keep up this pace we're on right now. It's not emotionally healthy for our family," Valentina said in a distressed voice, confiding her true feelings in her mother.

Isabella replied, "Valentina, this isn't about needing the money or not needing the money. This is about understanding what your husband needs as a man and honoring him as his wife. But most importantly, this is about Cortez seeing his papa fight through adversity and not give up, showing him what honor is all about. That's why I never agreed with Papa's stance on not allowing you to see his struggles. He taught you so many wonderful lessons about life, but the one lesson he never taught you was how to recover from a death blow after you've been knocked down – how to rebuild something that became damaged. That's what Takeo and Maria have been teaching their son Emilio through this more transparent way of parenting. How you choose to approach this challenging time will not only shape your son's character, but it will also shape your husband's. You need to help Vincent restore his honor."

But what about spending time with family? Isn't that what we worked so hard for?" Valentina asked.

"I fully understand what you're saying about the importance of spending time together as a family. That will always be important. But if you allow Vincent to walk away from the business knowing he just *gave up*, how will you look at him as a man? And even more importantly, how will he look at himself as a man? And how would you explain this to Cortez when he asks why his father isn't working anymore? Would you say, *'Well, he decided to stop working because it was too hard?'* You would undoubtedly have an easier life, yes. And that may make sense for some people, but Vincent isn't just *some people*, and neither are you. You are both people of honor. That's what Takeo and Maria were talking about tonight – the sixth virtue of the *Bushidō* code: *Meiyo* 名誉," Isabella said.

"But mama, Vincent has worked so hard. He needs a break. I'm… I'm worried about him. I just want him to be happy," Valentina said in a troubled voice as her eyes became glassy.

"Honey, to live a life focused on *purpose* instead of just *enjoyment* – on making an impact on others as opposed to just enjoying your *own* life – is part of what *honor* is all about. It's the understanding that an *easy life* isn't as fulfilling as a *life of significance*. I think this is an opportunity for you to teach your son something that Papa never taught you – how to bounce back, especially during times when life is not easy. But most importantly right now, you must help your husband rebuild his spirit and restore his honor because I can tell he's broken right now. This is what a queen does for her king. It won't be easy honey, but I'll help you through this process every step of the way," Isabella said, reaching over to give Valentina a strong reassuring hug.

After their conversation, Isabella and Valentina walked into the kitchen to help me clean up, but by that time, I had finished most of the dishes. Isabella kissed me on the forehead good night as she exited the kitchen. Valentina walked up behind me not saying a word, gently placing her arms around me, burying her left cheek into my upper back between my shoulder blades. I turned around and held her as she held me.

She whispered, "I'm so proud of you honey. It takes a real man to weather this kind of storm, and I know this hasn't been easy for you. However long it takes, I'm with you on this, okay?"

We sat down on the camel leather stools at the center island as Valentina shared with me everything Isabella just shared with her about The Icon's challenges and struggles. It was fascinating to learn so much history about a man that I thought I knew everything about already. It was hard for me to hear of these hardships and challenges The Icon endured, for I knew nothing about them despite how close we were.

After an hour-long deep conversation with Valentina, she headed off to bed as I took a walk out back by the pool. I thought about what Takeo said regarding letting Emilio see him struggle and fight through adversities. It was such a different approach to life than what The Icon believed in. The Icon didn't even share with his family that he was dying of pancreatic cancer until the very end. Isabella was the only one that knew. He never shared with me any of the problems he had with Andrei embarrassing him in the past. He also never shared with me his experience with Joan Gastineau, or the lawsuit, or any of his struggles. I wondered if he

137

had done his family a disservice by keeping them in the dark about his hardships. Perhaps had I known about some of The Icon's business struggles, I wouldn't have felt so badly about my own.

The more Takeo shared with me his past struggles, the more relatable he became to me – the more *human* he became to me. If anything, it brought us closer together. The Icon was an incredible mentor to me, but I always looked at him like he was super-human. In many ways, I didn't even look at him as a *human being* – rather half-man, half-deity – and perhaps that wasn't fair to either of us. I looked up to him so much because he was the father figure I never had, and he was also the business mentor I so desperately needed at that time – the business mentor I so desperately needed now to rebuild my company. The Icon lived a seemingly perfect life, but there is no such thing as a perfect life, or a perfect man for that matter. Perhaps I unfairly put him on a pedestal, and in doing so, it made me strive for perfection too, which was an unattainable goal.

With Takeo's explanations of the beauty of *kintsugi* and the ironic philosophy of the *wabi-sabi* aesthetic design, I began to accept the fact that a great life was not one void of struggles. In fact, there was an even greater beauty found in a damaged and repaired life.

I had certainly accomplished the *damaged* part, and now with the help of Takeo, I hoped to accomplish the *repaired* part as well. However *hoping* is not a strategy. I needed to continue to bare the unbearable, which at times felt like an exercise in futility, and during my weakest moments, I just felt like giving up on life.

But every time I came close to making terrible, irreversible decisions, Takeo was the one to talk me off the ledge.

Chapter 13
Know The Ledge

One night after one of our *Tabata* sessions at the *Secret Mesa Stairway*, I asked Takeo how he was able to find *his* extra gear during the turmoil of rebuilding his company. As we descended down the 201 stairs at the end of our workout, Takeo explained how he met the man who taught him the *Bushidō* code – Rob Charleston.

"Rob was a Caucasian guy from Northern California – fourteen years older than me – married to a beautiful Hawaiian gal named Cher. They had two young children – Mikey and Jolene. I met them when I was a broke college student in living in Hawaii. Back then, I had long hair down to my chest, two big hoop earrings, and I was a bouncer at a night club in Waikiki when I was going to school. I had only met the Charlestons a few times, but one night after a get together at a mutual friend's house, Rob pulled me into the other room and said, *'The Lord has blessed us with a house bigger than we need, and we have an extra bedroom that we're not using. I know you're in college and money's tight right now, so Cher and I would like to invite you to come stay with us, rent-free.'* I never told them this, but I went home and cried that night for hours. No one had ever extended themselves to me like that before. Here I was – a total stranger to them – and they invited me into their home to live with their family. Who does that?" Takeo said as his voice tapered into an emotional whisper.

We stopped on the 147th step as Takeo attempted to regain his composure. I had never seen Takeo get emotional like this before. He was always so stone-faced.

"They took me in and loved me like I was part of their family. I remember one night Rob saw me eating a big French baguette with some peanut butter on it for dinner, and he asked me, *'Are you eating that because you like it, or because you're trying to save money right now?'* I was so embarrassed, I just looked down at the floor and said nothing. Rob told me, *'From now on, you're going to join our family for dinner, okay?'* He said it in such a nonchalant way, as if it was no big deal. He had a way of giving me so much without making me feel uncomfortable. He was only fourteen years older than me, but he treated me like I was his own son," Takeo explained.

"Wow. They must have been pretty wealthy if they were your benefactors," I assumingly said.

Takeo stared off into the distance as his eyes became glassy. He nodded, but not in confirmation of my assessment. I could tell there was a deeper story behind this story because Takeo began to get choked up. I had never seen Takeo so emotionally moved like this. He was usually so stoic with this *half-samurai-half-Yoda* countenance, but whenever he talked about the Charlestons, he became extremely sentimental and emotional.

"Rob was a counselor at a high school for at-risk kids that were in and out of lock up, and Cher was an elementary school teacher at a private school. They are the richest family I know," Takeo said, motioning me to continue our descent down the stairs.

"The richest family you know? On a counselor's and teacher's salary? So they must have come from extremely wealthy families I'm assuming. Did they have an enormous trust fund or something?" I asked.

"I didn't say they were financially *wealthy*. I said they were *rich*. Rich in love. Rich in generosity. Rich in grace. They were rich in all the areas of life that truly matter. What they did for me went far beyond just giving me a roof over my head and feeding me, which was a big deal, don't get me wrong. But they gave me something that money can't buy: unconditional love. I was still an idiot back then – a recovering hot-head. I even got shot in a drive-by shooting just three years before I met them. Imagine a young couple inviting a stranger who just got shot in a drive-by shooting into their home to live with them and their two young children. And it wasn't just how they treated me. That was only one of countless blessings I received from them. I got to witness how a husband should treat his wife, and how a wife should treat her husband. I saw firsthand how parents should both love and discipline their children. I saw them help so many people that were struggling in their marriages, struggling with alcoholism, struggling with emotional problems – for nothing in return. Their living room was practically a counseling office as visitors came over to their house all the time to receive counseling and encouragement from Rob and Cher as I watched the kids in the back room. They taught me how to love people. So when I say they're the richest people I know, I'm not talking about material possessions. I'm talking about *true riches*. I've never been treated with such dignity and I've never felt more loved and accepted by anyone outside of my wife Maria," Takeo said as he reminisced over his relationship with his mentors.

Takeo loved Rob as one of his closest friends, but their friendship was not one between peers. Rob was like a father to Takeo despite their small age gap, and more accurately, Rob was like a sensei. The relationship dynamic between these two men became the most influential factor in developing Takeo into the man he would eventually become. Takeo revered Rob in the way that I revered The Icon – the way I grew to revere Takeo. But as much as Takeo loved Rob, he got even more emotional about Cher.

"Think about what that conversation must have been like between Rob and Cher when they made the decision to invite me to live with them. Do you think most young mothers want some thuggish looking stranger living in their home with her young children? Plus there was now another mouth to feed, not to mention having to deal with the lack of privacy with a stranger living in their home. Think about how inconvenient and uncomfortable that must have been for Cher as a woman. Think about the level of trust she placed in me. Think about how much faith in God she had in order to go along with all of this. You see, Cher set the blueprint for me as to the type of woman I wanted to marry because I saw the way she loved Rob. She let him lead their family, and even during times where she might have preferred that Rob handled certain things differently, she never challenged his male ego. And don't misunderstand what I'm saying. Cher was no pushover. She was strong, intelligent, and wise. She had her own career and was an independent woman, but she always made Rob feel like a *man*. She was so amazing, and I've always looked up to her as a big sister," Takeo said.

"It sounds like you're describing your wife, Maria," I said.

141

"Exactly. I wouldn't have the wife I have today if it wasn't for Cher setting this blueprint for me," Takeo said.

Takeo's relationship with Rob and Cher reminded me of my relationship with The Icon and Isabella. It was really something special – a bond that was truly spectacular.

"Rob also taught me martial arts and introduced me to the *Bushidō* code. Can you believe that? A *haole* guy teaching this Japanese guy about samurai culture?" Takeo said as he chuckled to himself.

He continued, "Back when they took me in to live with them, Rob and I would train almost every night in his car port. He would back the cars into the driveway, and we would train right there on the concrete. Rob was a very accomplished ex-professional mixed martial artist who fought for the PRIDE organization in front of over thirty thousand people in *Saitama Super Arena* in Japan in his early thirties. The style Rob taught me was decades ahead of its time. It was a combination of boxing, aikido, judo, and jiu-jitsu. But Rob's goal wasn't to teach me how to fight. His goal was to use martial arts as a way to teach me more about his faith in a way that I would relate to. Rob taught me about Christianity by weaving it into the seven virtues of the *Bushidō* code. He knew that my enthusiasm towards learning about my Japanese/samurai culture and martial arts would be greater than talking about the Bible, so that's how he got me to open up to him, and as a result of his more palatable evangelism style, I became a much stronger Christian. He taught me that samurai take their duty so seriously, they put their duty above their own lives. Well, that's what Rob and Cher did for me. They believed their duty in life was to use the gifts that God gave them to help other people, despite how that might inconvenience their own personal lives. One of my favorite Bible verses is John 15:13 that says, '*No greater love hath a man than he lay down his own life for his friends.*' Rob often used this quote to reinforce virtue #7 of the *Bushidō* code: Chūgi 忠義, which means *loyalty*. To everyone samurai were responsible for, they remained fiercely true, and they were willing to lay down their lives for the people they pledged their loyalty to. The Charlestons laid down their lives for me, and I'll spend the rest of my life indebted to them. Rob literally saved my life," Takeo said.

I paused for a moment to let all of this sink in, but there was something in the way Takeo said that last part that sounded incomplete.

"Umm, when you say Rob *saved your life…* uh…"

"Vincent, when I faced the betrayal of my employees and my business started crumbling to the ground, I was in a bad place. I mean *really bad*. I've been teaching you the virtues of the *Bushidō* code, and perhaps you think that I have a certain level of emotional strength, but this is something that I had to work really hard at. When I went through that period of betrayal and rebuilding, I took a business trip out to Honolulu to try to form an alliance with a couple of firms that were international investment hubs for the Japanese and Chinese markets. While I was there, I obviously went to visit Rob and Cher," said Takeo.

I could tell he was about to share something very intimate with me – something that I would relate to.

"I really needed those meetings to go well, and they did not go well at all. I had spent months and months trying to put a deal together with them prior to my trip out there. I was right there on the one-yard line with them, and at the end of both of those meetings, they informed me that they decided to go in a different direction. I was hemorrhaging so much negative cash flow each month, I couldn't even pay my bills on time. I had everything riding on those meetings. I took Rob and Cher to dinner that night, and two of my credit cards got declined – unbeknownst to me, they were completely maxed out – and Rob and Cher had to pay for dinner. I was absolutely mortified," Takeo explained as we reached the bottom of the stairs.

He paused and took a deep inhale and slowly exhaled as we stood on the sidewalk facing each other, but this was not *kata* breathing. His exhale was troubled, uneven, and was definitely not calming.

Takeo continued, "That next morning, I drove up the Pali Highway – a highway that connects the South Shore of Oahu to the

East side of the Island. It starts out in Downtown Honolulu, wraps up into the mountains and drops you off in Kailua, right where Rob and Cher's house was. I stopped at the *Pali Lookout* – the midpoint that overlooks the East side of the island. I got out of the car, walked beyond the guard rails, and knelt down right on the ledge," Takeo said.

I knew what he was about to tell me. I could see it in his eyes. There is a feeling of despair that runs so deep, it makes you feel as though you are beyond redemption. I knew that feeling intimately, for that was exactly how I was feeling in that moment.

"Rob was on his way to work that Wednesday morning, driving from Kailua to Honolulu on the Pali, and he saw my rental car parked at the lookout. He turned into the parking lot and pulled up next to my car. Something in Rob's spirit told him to get out and venture down the cliff in search of me. And there I was, kneeling at the edge of the cliff with a large knife in my hand, ready to commit *seppuku*," Takeo explained in an unstable and uneasy voice – a voice very atypical from the Takeo I knew.

Seppuku was a Japanese ritualistic way to commit suicide. Takeo was such a strong man with such a strong spirit and Zen-like countenance, it was difficult for me to imagine him this distraught. It was a reminder that he was indeed human – a human being that once had the same troubled soul that I had.

"Takeo, you don't want to do this brother," Rob said in a stern yet compassionate voice.

Takeo didn't make eye contact with Rob. His pride would not allow him to do so. He just continued to stare off into the horizon from edge of the cliff.

"They took everything from me! I can't pay my bills, man! I haven't paid my mortgage in nine months! I've failed everyone around me! Everything I've worked for is now gone! Fourteen years of work… all gone! Chūgi 忠義 doesn't exist, man! There's no such thing as *loyalty*! Everyone has betrayed me!" Takeo shouted.

At that moment in Takeo's life, he had trained under Rob for over twenty years. As I did the math, I realized this only happened seven years ago. I couldn't fathom this amazingly strong, seemingly bulletproof samurai warrior reaching that level of hopelessness. Despite Takeo's years of *Bushidō* training and faith in God, it was proof that everyone is susceptible to feelings of despair and hopelessness, completely losing perspective.

"*Everyone* has betrayed you?" questioned Rob in his calm, compassionate voice. "*Everyone*, including Maria? *Everyone*, including me and Cher?"

Takeo looked at Rob as tears ran down his cheeks.

Rob took a one step closer to Takeo.

"Have I betrayed you Takeo?" asked Rob.

"That's not what I mean, and you know it!" yelled Takeo.

"Has Cher betrayed you? And what about Maria? Has your wife betrayed you?" Rob calmly asked.

Takeo just stared at Rob as his sobbing began to subside.

Rob took two steps closer to Takeo.

"We've all had people betray us. Even Jesus. Listen, what those people did to you was wrong. You did nothing to deserve that. But remember *Job* in the Bible? Remember what happened to him? Even his own wife turned against him, telling him he should curse God and die. Is that what Maria is telling you?" Rob asked, knowing darn well Maria's undying love for Takeo would never allow her to say anything of the sort.

"I have brought shame to my family! I have failed them! I have dishonored them! Harakiri is the only way out! Death before dishonor!" Takeo yelled in a thunderously loud and distraught voice.

"Whoa, whoa. Slow down brother. Takeo, there's nothing honorable about doing this. Your son needs you Takeo. Emilio needs his father. And Maria is the best thing that ever happened to you. She's as loyal as loyal gets, and if you really do lose your entire fortune, she's going to stick with you through thick and thin. You know this. And so what if you lose everything? You built a very successful company once before. That means you can rebuild

145

it again. I know you can do it, and so does Maria," Rob encouragingly said.

Takeo's strong grip on the handle of his knife became slightly looser, and in a defeated and very unconfident voice, he softly replied, "And what if I can't? What if I don't have what it takes?"

I couldn't imagine the Takeo I knew doubting himself like that, but again, it was a reminder that he was indeed human.

"First of all, I know you have what it takes. I know what you're made of, and you're not a quitter. You've made great decisions all the way up until this point in your life. Don't stop now. Put that knife down, brother. Please," Rob calmly said, taking three more steps closer to Takeo.

In that same defeated voice, Takeo said, "But what if I can't rebuild? What if I can't do it?"

"You don't have to do it all by yourself, Takeo. Did you do it all by yourself the first time?" asked Rob.

"You know I did."

"Really? You did it the first time, *all* by yourself?"

"Yeah man. No one helped me. No one set me up for success. I had to build it from nothing. Just me," Takeo said.

"You see Takeo, that's where you're wrong. You're amazingly smart and talented, no doubt about it. But no one achieves the level of success you've achieved all on their own. God created opportunities for you to succeed. Yes, you worked hard. You're the most disciplined, hard-working man I know when it comes to business. But you would be nothing without God's favor. And if God came through for you once, He can do it again, but you've got to trust Him and surrender. You don't have to do any of this 100% on your own. Chūgi 忠義 isn't about loyalty between men. We all know that men will let us down from time to time, but God's loyalty towards us is everlasting. His love is unconditional. He'll help you get through this Takeo. You just have to surrender and let Him lead the way," Rob rationalized.

Rob didn't pull Takeo off the ledge. He didn't wrestle the knife out of his hands. He didn't force an embrace either. Rob just opened his arms to Takeo. He wanted Takeo to make the decision put down his knife, come down off the ledge, and choose to embrace him on his own.

This was the wisdom of Rob Charleston.

It was an unsaid gesture, analogous to the way God loves us. God never forces His love on us, but rather He invites us to surrender – to drop our egos, our insecurities, and our troubles – and come to Him on our own will, just as we are, imperfections and all. That was what Rob did for Takeo.

Takeo looked at Rob with his arms open wide, ready to receive him. He looked down the steep cliff, then looked at Rob, then looked down the steep cliff again for several seconds. He regripped the knife tightly in his hands, trembling as he reconsidered the irreversible decision he was about to make just before Rob showed up on the cliff to meet him.

"Takeo, look at me, brother. Please," Rob said in a calm, soothing and compassionate voice.

Takeo slowly turned his head to see Rob.

"Takeo, I will help you through this. No matter how bad things get in life, I will always be in your corner. You have my loyalty, always, no matter what. Please come down. Come on brother, you're gonna make me late for work. You don't want your big brother to get fired from his job now, do you?" Rob asked with a smile.

And with Rob's disarming humor, just like that, Takeo started laughing.

Sometimes the most beautiful and joyous feeling a human being can experience is when tears of despair are interrupted by laughter. It is the reminder that no matter how bad things may appear, there are still remnants of joy in our lives that we have temporarily lost sight of. Rob's gentle reminder was all it took to break Takeo out of his dark emotional state.

Rob was a talented counselor and his profession certainly allowed him to build the skills to calm people down and reach them at the emotional level. He was a master at helping people remember what was important, and not to take anything away from Rob's counseling skills, but I truly believe that encounter involved quite a bit of divine intervention that day. God knew the world needed Takeo, and perhaps He knew that one day, years later, I would need Takeo too.

There was no greater human example of *Bushidō* code, virtue #7: *Chūgi/Loyalty* being exemplified than the relationship between Takeo and Rob. Rob's commitment to mentoring Takeo was deeply ingrained in his spirit, the way a father shoulders his responsibility of mentoring his son.

But Takeo's commitment to honor his relationship with Rob and Cher seemed to affect me at the visceral level in a bittersweet way. It was this kind of loyalty that I had towards The Icon, Joseph, Francisco, and now Takeo, for they had given me so much. But when I thought about how much I had given Kane, the lack of reciprocation just enraged me. I was still so bitter and resentful.

I wanted to replicate this mentor/mentee relationship with Kane and have the same deep bond I shared with my mentors – to have this foundational *Chūgi/Loyalty* quality. I shared so many intimate secrets with Kane as I attempted to create this special bond, which is why his betrayal hurt me so deeply. I vowed to never open myself up to anyone like that again ever again. Yet despite Takeo going through the same type of betrayal, there he was opening himself up to me as his mentee. As Takeo shared this part of his life with me, I could tell this wasn't something he shared with just anyone. Up until that point, he and Rob were the only ones that knew about this encounter. Not Maria. Not Cher. Just Takeo and Rob... and now me.

I looked at Takeo, admiring his courage to share with me such an intimate and dark moment in his life, and mumbled, "And what if I can't?"

"Can't what?" Takeo asked.

"What if I can't recover? What if I can't reinvent myself like you did? I love everything you're teaching me about the *Bushidō* code, but I'm not as tough as you," I ashamedly admitted as my breathing rapidly increased with a panicked cadence. My eyes became red as I fought to hold back tears.

"Vincent, I've been there. I get it."

"But you're a *samurai*, man. I'm not. I'm just a scrawny kid from a crappy little town in Kansas who got pummeled by Andrei and Michael. Do you know how embarrassing that was for me, man? My wife and son saw me in the emergency room all busted up. They broke my arm, my back, AND my jaw," I admitted.

"Are you saying you literally got physically assaulted? I had no idea," Takeo said, confused and surprised, yet compassionate and empathetic.

I hadn't shared that experience with him yet. As I told him what happened in their office, I buried my face in my forearms, covering up my tears so that Takeo couldn't see what an emotional mess I was. Despite me knowing that Takeo had been through similar struggles – perhaps even more tumultuous than mine – I was still ashamed and embarrassed. It was a level of loneliness that no man can accurately articulate, yet I know many men have felt this kind of despair at one time or another in their lives, and though I knew I was not alone in feeling like this, I certainly felt alone. I was falling apart, thought by thought, cell by cell. I could feel my spirit disintegrating, and the ground felt like it was crumbling beneath me.

"I don't know if I'm gonna make it to the end of this month, man. My credit cards are all maxed out, and I'm three months behind on paying my office rent. I don't think I can hold it together much longer. I got nothing left man... I got nothing... I... I got..." I couldn't even finish my sentence as I gasped for air, trying to catch my breath as I struggled to speak through my hyperventilating.

Takeo quickly grabbed me by the triceps, holding me up, preventing me from collapsing, saying, "Okay, okay, okay. Look here Vincent, that's nothing to be ashamed of or embarrassed about.

No one's ever taught you how to defend yourself, and no one's ever taught you how to rebuild a damaged business either. I'm going to teach you how to do both. I'm going to give you my entire playbook and coach you every step of the way, just like Rob did for me. And by the way, you might not come from a lineage of samurai warriors, but that doesn't mean you can't learn the discipline... and it doesn't mean that you don't have the same level of greatness inside of you. If Francisco believes in you, that's good enough for me. Listen, let's reconnect tomorrow night. It's time to begin the cleansing process."

Not fully understanding what Takeo meant by the term *cleansing process*, we exchanged a half-handshake-half-hug, but this time, he held me for just a moment longer, just like Francisco always did. He knew I needed it.

He then said, "I have something for you."

Takeo walked over to his *Bronco* and grabbed an envelope out of the glove box with my name written on it and handed it to me.

"Read this tonight and we'll talk tomorrow evening," Takeo said as he departed.

As he drove off, I sat down on the curb and opened the envelope. Inside was a handwritten letter from Takeo to me.

Dear Vincent,

There are great life lessons embedded in fishing.

During the first three years of taking my son Emilio fishing, we never caught a single fish. A couple weeks ago, we went fishing again... and still, nothing. For three years, I would catch glimpses of him clasping his hands, eyes closed, praying to God to help him catch a fish. On these fishing expeditions, I talked to him about how winners have the unique ability to continue their pursuit with no less enthusiasm, despite having no signs of progress.

There are three key lessons I wanted to teach my son, and these are the same key lessons you need to embrace during this challenging time of yours:

1. *The greatest victories typically come after years of struggle. Embrace the struggle, knowing that your victory is in the making.*

2. *Those who face greater adversity often become far more talented. Calm seas have never produced a master sailor.*

3. *Delayed success often times allows us to ask God for help, so when success finally materializes, we know we can't take 100% credit. It forces us to acknowledge God's hand in our success. This keeps us humble.*

Truth be told, I don't even like fishing. It's just not my thing. But I love spending time with my son, regardless of what we're doing together. He happens to love fishing, so that's what we do together.

I love teaching him life lessons that will benefit him in his future life struggles. It is my job to teach him how to deal with disappointment and challenging times. I must teach my son to accept the uncertainty of the future, yet approach each attempt with the same vigor and positive enthusiasm, especially when he is tired, and even more so when he has racked up a string of consecutive failures. This is a way of approaching life from a process-driven mindset, as opposed to an outcome-driven mindset.

Two weeks ago, I told my son how proud I was of him for his continued enthusiasm despite our three years of unsuccessful fishing. I told him that in life, he must focus on the process, not the outcome – and in this case, that he must focus on "fishing" instead of "catching."

I even taught him an acronym. N.A.T.O. – Not Attached To Outcomes. It's a lesson that even I have to remind myself of.

Ironically, the very next weekend, Emilio caught his first fish! He was so excited. I captured it on video and everything. But the reason he appreciated that victory so deeply was that he knew what it felt like to "fail" for the first three years. It taught him that there is no such thing as overnight success, and that sometimes, things take much longer than we want them to.

It can be a lonely feeling when you are going through tough times. Sometimes it feels like you're the only one going through it. Sometimes it makes you feel like there is something wrong with you, and sometimes it makes you feel like a failure.

As you now know, I have been there too.

I wanted to share my experience with Rob at the top of the Pali lookout with you for two main reasons.

1. *You are not alone in feeling the way you do.*
2. *I am not perfect.*

I was once lost, just like you are right now, and if it wasn't for Rob, perhaps I wouldn't be here today.

You will get through this, just as I did. You will be triumphant, just like I have been, and I am committed to going the distance with you, just as Rob was for me.

Your Friend,

Takeo

Chapter 14
Going The Distance

The next evening, I met Takeo at his home in Orange County. He let me know ahead of time that we would be doing a much more difficult type of workout, so I uploaded a playlist of my favorite workout songs to my phone. As I started to lace up my gym shoes, I put in my earbuds, and queued up my playlist.

"What are you doing?" Takeo questioned.

"What do you mean?" I asked.

"You don't need your earbuds. We're not going to listen to music during this session. Go ahead and put that way," Takeo said.

"But I use this to pump me up," I explained.

Takeo looked at me and smiled, slowly shaking his head with respectful disapproval.

"Vincent, you say you *need* the music to pump you up – to get you in the right emotional state so you can push yourself harder if I'm understanding you, right?" Takeo asked, seeking confirmation.

"Is there something wrong with listening to motivational music when we're working out?" I questioned.

Takeo replied, "Let me ask you something. You say you *need* this music to pump you up, right?"

"Yeah, but…"

"Vincent, what happens in real life when you don't have the music to pump you up, when you're all alone and it's just you and your thoughts?" Takeo asked.

"Umm…"

"Do you think I'm having you workout with me because I think you need six-pack abs or to win a professional *CrossFit* championship?" Takeo asked.

"Of course not."

"So why do you think I'm teaching you these workouts?" Takeo asked.

Similar to The Icon, Takeo never told me what to do. Instead, he would either teach me through analogous storytelling, or he would help me discover the answers on my own by asking me a series of questions that drilled down into the core of the lesson.

"I suppose it's to teach me how to push through pain?" I answered in a tone that made it sound like more of a question than a statement.

"Vincent, *Tabata* training is a great cardiovascular workout, but the real training embedded in *Tabata* protocol is the mental game. Towards the end of the workout, you should be gasping for every breath you take, and each time you begin another twenty seconds of torture, the challenge should be so great that you have to talk yourself into continuing. This is the same thing you have to do when you're facing challenges in business the way you are right now. You have to dig deep into your core – not just in your mind, but your soul and spirit – and literally talk yourself into pushing harder, especially when you feel like you have nothing left in the tank. You need to find that extra gear," Takeo said.

"So listening to pump-me-up music is cheating?" I asked.

"I don't know if I would call it *cheating*, but it makes you rely on an external source for motivation. For me, when I hit that wall in my *Tabata* workouts, I start having motivational conversations with myself. In the Bible, it talks about Kind David having to give himself pep talks. 1 Samuel 30:6 says, *'And David was greatly distressed; for the people spoke of stoning him... but David encouraged himself in the Lord his God.'* Sometimes you have to encourage yourself when there's no one there to encourage you – not me, not Jay-Z, not a Rocky Balboa soundtrack – when it's just you and God," Takeo explained.

I never thought about workouts in this manner. I always thought the goal of the workout was to just get physically stronger, burn fat, and get into better shape. Takeo was in incredible shape, but I learned that *Tabata* training was his method of mental training, not just extreme cardio training.

This further explained why he loved training at the *Secret Mesa Stairway*. 201 steps – not 200 – 201 steps. He wasn't interested in being a *champion*. He was committed to *mastery*. His intensity during these workout sessions was really something to watch. I never saw anyone push themselves harder than Takeo, and he attacked each interval was like it was his last. Each effort was 100% of his best, and even after climbing 200 steps and hitting his VO2 max, he found the strength to climb one last unnecessary extra step, just to prove to himself that despite his maximum effort, he could go beyond what the lactic acid in his quads, hamstrings, and calves told him. I came to realize that this wasn't merely due to his aerobic endurance or his anaerobic strength. His real strength was in his mind and in his spirit. He had the ability to bear the unbearable, and that's what I needed to learn to do – bear the unbearable.

We walked out to Takeo's Noguchi-inspired rock garden towards the entrance of the property as he instructed me to sit cross-legged facing each other.

"I thought we were doing *Tabata* tonight," I said.

"This is a different type of exercise – much harder than *Tabata*. First off, let's close our eyes and be still," Takeo calmly instructed.

Takeo's neighborhood was incredibly quiet. Each property sat on an acre-plus lot, and at Takeo's home, the only thing you could hear at night were the crickets and the gentle sound of the stream running through his rock garden.

"Take in a deep breath, filling your lungs to their maximum capacity. Now and hold your breath for twenty seconds," instructed Takeo.

After twenty seconds, he said, "Now exhale slowly for ten seconds, extinguishing every last bit of air out of your lungs. Okay, again. Inhale slowly and deeply to your maximum lung capacity and hold for twenty."

This was the same ratio as the *Tabata* workouts we had been doing, but in this exercise, it was just breathing.

"We're cleansing our lymphatic system. Our lymphatic system provides many different immune functions that protect us from infections and viruses. Unlike our blood circulation that's propelled by the pumping of our heart, our lymphatic system has no pump of its own, so the circulation of our lymphatic fluid from our lymphatic vessels to our lymph nodes is generated by two main things: movement and deep diaphragmatic breathing, which is what we're doing right now. This helps us to eliminate toxins from our system," Takeo explained.

The more I learned about Takeo's exercise methods, I came to realize that the health benefits were *side benefits*. The primary reason he chose these methods had more to do with the mental, emotional, and spiritual benefits – a way to build something strong from within, and also to cleanse himself of all negative thoughts and emotions.

With each inhale, he said, "Visualize God's love and positive energy entering your body through your nose, down into your lungs, and seeping into your gut. This is your source of power. Each inhalation is filling your body, mind, and soul with His love and power. We hold our breath for twenty seconds to let that love and power circulate through our entire body, and when we exhale, we extinguish every last ounce of negativity, stress, and worry from our body. As you think about all the negativity leaving your body, visualize certain people that have caused you pain. As you see their faces, say out loud to them, *'I forgive you,'* and let it all go. All of it."

I had heard about the power of *letting go*, but it wasn't until that moment wherein I fully understood what that meant. Sometimes we become so used to holding on to resentment that it becomes an addiction, as if we almost *need* to feel angry about something to make us feel relevant. But this addiction – like most addictions – prevents you from ever having a joyful heart. As I audibly said *'I forgive you'* to these people, it literally felt like someone was slowly removing rocks from a 100-pound backpack I had been carrying around on my shoulders since my childhood. I didn't realize what I was doing to myself all those years, allowing other people to load up this backpack – rock by rock – giving them permission to weigh me down. With each *'I forgive you'* that accompanied the exhale I released, each rock that weighed me down was removed, one by one. I can't explain it, but after feeling so *heavy* all these years, I never felt so *light* and free. It was liberating.

"Vincent, this is where you need to trust God. God allowed these people to come into your life. He put them there to teach you lessons. Sometimes we need to experience ultimate heartbreak in order to fully appreciate true love. If your ex-wife was responsible for your heartbreak, then in an indirect way, she was also responsible for you finding Valentina. What she did *for* you by leaving you was one of the greatest blessings in your entire life. In fact, she didn't *leave* you. She *released* you to fulfill your true destiny and to find your true love in Valentina," Takeo said.

I thought about Takeo's words. He said what she did *for* me – not *to* me, but *for* me. I had been holding on to anger and resentment related to these betrayals, when I should really be writing these people thank you notes. Without my ex-wife's betrayal, I wouldn't be married to Valentina. Without Kane and Andrei's betrayal, I wouldn't have my friendship with Takeo.

Then Takeo said, "Once you have forgiven everyone who has harmed you, there is one last person you need to forgive."

I knew what Takeo was going to say next. That last person I needed to forgive was myself. This was the hardest one by far. I couldn't seem to let go of my own self-inflicted guilt due to reaching a level of self-hatred that had completely overtaken my soul. It was very dark and very ugly, and though I realized how much it was destroying me from within – similar to watching cancer spread throughout one's body – it felt like there was nothing I could do about it. Takeo could tell this was my greatest challenge because he too had experienced these feelings of self-hatred firsthand.

"Vincent, I know you blame yourself for all of this financial turmoil you're going through now, but you're giving yourself too much credit," Takeo said.

"Too much credit? What do you mean?" I asked.

"God is creating a void in your business right now to create space for growth. You're being pruned, just like the lime tree I told you about when you came to my office. If you believe that this pruning is setting you up for greater success than you've ever had, you can't take credit for this blessing. I know it may not feel like a blessing right now, and I know it probably feels like a curse, but this is all part of the plan – part of the cycle. If you blame yourself for the fungus on your lime tree, and you're angry at God for cutting off all the leaves and buds, then in a sense, you're trying to take 100% credit for the massive lime harvest that's coming your way," Takeo explained.

"But how do you know there's a harvest coming my way?" I asked.

"This is where faith comes in – believing in something that you can't see. For example, it's 9:00 p.m. right now, which means the sun won't rise for another ten hours or so, but you have faith that it will, right? It doesn't look like it will because we're sitting here in the dark right now, but you believe that the sun will rise tomorrow morning, and we'll be blessed with another day. The question is, in the midst of being in this dark place in your business right now, *'Do you believe that the sun will indeed rise again?'* Your answer to this question is what defines your faith," Takeo said.

Reframing my own guilt, realizing that I was actually taking *credit* for what my destiny held, was such a radical revelation for me. All of this burden I was carrying on my shoulders was in direct conflict with what I had already personally experienced in my life. Every void created in my life that was refilled by something better was certainly not refilled by me. They were refilled by God.

At times, I lost my faith in God, and if I'm being completely honest with myself, during these times of extreme hardship, I questioned whether God even existed at all. But by cathartically reliving these hardships and realizing what came as a result of them, I was reunited with the fact that *someone* refilled these voids. If it wasn't God, were these void-filling blessings just a coincidence?

For someone that doesn't believe in God, I suppose they could chalk these events up to a series of coincidences, however that would be an awful lot of coincidences and an awful lot of coincidental dots that coincidentally connected in a beautiful way.

"Okay Vincent. Next up is our gratitude exercise. I want you to think of three things you're grateful for. The first one is simple. Think of one person who has contributed so much to your life that they either changed it, created it, or saved it. Think about your love for them, and their love for you. And think of one specific moment when they were really there for you in your time of need. Relive that moment. What did they look like? What were they wearing? How did they smell? What did their voice sound like? How did they make you feel? Relive that moment, and say *'Thank you. I love you.'* Say it out loud," Takeo instructed.

I remember so vividly the first time The Icon and Isabella invited me to their home for dinner. They took such a special interest in me, listening to me as I expressed the angst I had over my troubled relationship with my father. I was so grateful for my relationship with both of them, for they opened their home to me and opened their hearts to me back when I felt like nobody loved me. They set me on the path of discovering an entirely different world and an entirely different way of living. Not to take anything away from how much I valued my relationship with Isabella, but The Icon was the father figure I never had. I missed him so much. I audibly said in a faint whisper, "Thank you. I love you. I miss you," as my voice mildly trembled. I missed him so much, yet in that moment, my feelings of sorrow were so massively overridden by my feelings of appreciation and gratitude for the blessing he was in my life.

Then Takeo said, "Next, I want you to think about something that happened to you – a coincidence or a random event – something that could have easily not have happened that led to a blessing. Sometimes things happen in our lives that we think are coincidences, but they are not coincidental at all. They're all part of a divine intervention – God's plan. We may not fully understand them when they're occurring, and they may seem random and insignificant, but think of a time one of these coincidences happened that became a major blessing in your life. But most of all, recognize that this so-called random encounter was something that you did nothing to deserve. It wasn't *earned*. I just happened *for* you."

I thought about meeting Valentina for the first time at *Madre's Coffee* and thinking that would be the last time I would ever see her, then *randomly* reuniting with her in New York. But as Takeo explained, these events were not random at all. These were clearly divine interventions, for my life would be so incomplete without her. No other woman could have handled me the way Valentina did. She knew how to get through to me without damaging my male ego. She was loving and understanding towards me even during times when my own behavior didn't deserve it, and to think that this incredible woman would *coincidentally* be revealed to me as the daughter of my mentor, The Icon.

There was nothing coincidental about my life – blessings upon blessings upon blessings – yet there I was in a state of diminished faith, focusing on the impossibility of rebuilding my company. However, in the midst of meditating on my gratitude towards Valentina, I was flooded by so many recollections of other so-called coincidences that were major pivotal moments in my life. So many times, we don't realize the impact of certain blessings as we are experiencing them. It is only long after these events occur that we can connect the dots and realize that life was happening *for* us all along – not *to* us, but *for* us.

Then Takeo said, "Lastly, I want you to focus on something that happened that seemed awful at first, where you thought it was the end of the world, but as time unfolded, you came to realize that it was the best thing that could have ever happened to you."

I immediately thought about that Sunday afternoon when my ex-wife Amber told me she wanted a divorce. She had come home from the gym as I was sitting on the couch in our living room, answering emails.

As she entered the living room, I could hear the friction between the soles of her shoes and the carpet. She slowly came to a stop, standing there in silence, staring at the floor.

"Vincent, we need to talk."

I kept working… *hearing*, but not really *listening*.

"Vincent. I've given this a lot of thought over the last few weeks, and I've made up my mind, so please don't try to talk me out of it."

I put my laptop computer down and sat up, looking at her with perturbed irritation.

"Vincent, I don't want to be married to you anymore."

"What... what do you mean?"

"Look Vincent, I can't do this anymore. I can't live like this. I'm tired of worrying about making next month's rent. I'm tired of just barely getting by every month. I can't take it. You're always telling me..."

"Wait a minute!" I argumentatively snapped. "I thought we were in this together! I thought we talked about this! No one gets rich overnight! Stuff like this takes time, and I've got this deal I'm working on, and it's really coming together. I'm really close to..."

"That's just it Vincent! You've always got some *deal* you're working on, and it's always some pie-in-the-sky get-rich-quick scheme, and..."

"What do you want me to do? Quit? Give up on my dream and go back to my old crappy job? I can't do that! I *won't* do that! I will *never* do that!"

"Vincent, it's..."

"Look, we can go to marriage counseling. I won't give up on my dream, and I won't give up on our marriage either. Whatever needs to be done – whatever changes I need to make – we can get through this. Tomorrow morning, I'll call Pastor Keith. I'll find out when he can see us and..."

"Vincent," she paused. "It's... it's over."

"No! Don't say that! We can..."

"Vincent, stop! I've already made up my mind and..."

"It's NOT over! We can make it work!" I desperately yelled at the top of my lungs.

"Please! I'll do anything you want," I pleaded.

I scrambled for the right words.

There was another long, awkward moment of silence that felt like it lasted a millennium.

Then I softly uttered, "Please don't leave me. Please."

She just stared across the room, looking right past me, as if I didn't exist.

"Please, just give me one more…"

"Vincent… it's over," she said, interrupting me in a faint, distracted whisper of a voice.

I interjected, "Please! Just one more chance. I'll…"

"Vincent!" she exclaimed with finality.

As her gaze past me turned into a deep stare into my soul, her eyes looked at me with pity. And as a man, there's nothing worse than to be looked upon with pity… especially by a woman.

It was emasculating.

I had lost all my confidence as a man, not that I had much to begin with. Amber had been my girlfriend since my Junior Year in college, and she was the first long-term relationship I had ever had. When she left, it felt like my life was over. It sounds crazy to hear myself say that given what my life has become since those days of old, back when I lived in that very small world. And now I found myself trying to build something from nothing again, focusing on what I had lost instead of focusing on what I stood to gain from all of this turmoil. If the void in my life created by my divorce opened the door for me to meet Valentina, then it would make logical sense for me to have faith that this void created by Andrei and Kane was an opportunity to build something even better as well.

I couldn't connect the dots yet, but Takeo helped me consider that this horrible situation I found myself in might actually be a blessing in disguise. That's what this mediation exercise was all about. Inhaling goodness and exhaling toxins wasn't just a lymphatic cleansing exercise. It was a cleansing of the soul. I even learned to embrace what Kane and Andrei had done because it ultimately resulted in me meeting my new mentor and friend – Takeo.

I learned that there would be no soundtrack or live band playing for me to cheer me on or motivate me in real life. I would have to encourage myself as King David did. Finding the extra gear that Takeo talked about had nothing to do with endurance, skill, or testicular fortitude. The real secret was rooted in my confidence of knowing that the outcome wouldn't define me – that I would instead be defined by how I navigated through challenges like a samurai warrior.

By letting go of my attachments, my embarrassment, and my ego, I began learning how to surrender to God and His plan for my life, despite how awful things appeared on the surface. There was a real freedom in submitting to this belief. It gave me the extra energy I needed – the extra gear Takeo had talked about – even after I thought I had extinguished every last bit of effort within me.

This belief – *that I didn't get this damn far JUST to get this damn far* – gave me everything I needed to go the distance, and for the first time in a long time, I knew I was gonna fly now.

Chapter 15
Gonna Fly Now

Takeo had me addicted to *Tabata* workouts and gratitude meditations. They strengthened my body and my mind, and also calmed my spirit. But one evening, Takeo brought a pair of boxing gloves and a pair of punch mitts to our workout, saying, "We're going to incorporate some basic *Mixed Martial Arts* into our training tonight, if that's okay with you."

After taking a beating from Andrei and Michael, this was something that I wanted to learn, but I was too embarrassed to ever inquire about it. Takeo's proposition came right on time. Perhaps sharing with him my embarrassment of getting pulverized by Andrei was a good thing. I put on the gloves and Takeo put on the punch mitts. As I stood there facing him, I felt exactly the same way I felt in my business at that time – unprepared and ill-equipped. My fingers fidgeted inside my gloves as I rocked my weight back into my heels, feeling uneasy and unconfident.

"Okay Vincent, we're going to start out with a little foot work and a basic punch sequence. Go ahead and get into a fighter's stance. I'm going to put up my pads, palms facing you. We're going to start off simple. When I say *One,* you're going to throw a short jab, hitting my left mitt with your left glove, and when you do that, you're going to push off your right foot and take a small step towards me with your left foot. Okay, *One,* " Takeo instructed.

I threw my jab as hard as I could, embarrassed that it wouldn't be hard enough. Takeo was such a powerful man in so many ways, and I felt weak and inadequate. At this point, I did as much as I could to overcompensate for my inadequacies.

"No, no, no. Don't wind up and unload like that. Don't try to *muscle* the punch. Just a light, quick jab. Pop it straight forward and tap my mitt, then retract it as fast as possible, putting your guard back up. In fact, I want you to focus more on how quickly you can retract the punch back into your chamber position than how hard you throw the punch. Okay, *One,* " Takeo said.

I snapped a light, crisp jab that barely tapped Takeo's punch mitt, then retracted it as quickly as I could, just as Takeo instructed.

"Good. Again. *One*," Takeo said.

I snapped another jab.

"Good. Very good. Now when I say *Two*, I want you to throw a right cross to my right mitt. Okay, let's start out a with a left jab again. *One*," Takeo prompted.

I popped my left jab.

"Good. *One, two*," said Takeo.

I through my combo. Pop, pop.

"Again. *One, two*."

Pop, pop.

"Excellent. Again. *One, two*."

Pop, pop.

I started getting hyped. I envisioned Andrei's face on those punch mitts and started punching harder and harder. My adrenaline was surging as I began to flashback to the altercation in Kane's office. I even started grunting as I punched harder and harder.

"Whoa, whoa, whoa. You're winding up again, trying to power punch. The key to an effective jab is it's got to follow a linear path. Straight in, straight out. When you wind up and throw your punches from behind the shoulder, your opponent can react because they see the punch coming. Don't telegraph your punches. It doesn't matter how hard your punches are if they don't land. It's just like in business. Swinging hard doesn't get the job done as well as a series of well executed precision punches. Precision beats power. Timing beats speed. You have to remember that the *knockout punch* isn't necessarily the *hardest* punch you throw. It's the *right timed* punch that your opponent doesn't see coming," Takeo explained.

Every lesson Takeo taught me was analogous to another area of my life. When he taught me about *kintsugi*, he was teaching me how to repair my spirit. When he taught me about *Tabata* workouts, he was teaching me how to overcome myself. And when he was training me in *Mixed Martial Arts*, he was really teaching me about business strategy. Our *Secret Mesa Stairs* workouts continued but were far less frequent, as we transitioned into doing more and more *MMA-style* workouts at Takeo's home. Many of my family's weekends were spent at Takeo's home where the wives and Isabella would cook together, our sons would play together, and Takeo and I would train together.

I had been carrying the burden of feeling weak and helpless after I got beat down by Andrei, and that feeling of weakness subconsciously bled into my business. It is very difficult for a man to feel weak in body, yet strong in mind and spirit. Incongruency and authenticity cannot reside within a man's spirit simultaneously.

After several months, my aerobic and anaerobic strength began to climb rapidly, and I had dropped twenty-two pounds of body fat off of my dad-bod. I didn't quite have a six-pack yet, but my four-pack was chiseling in quite nicely. In addition, my confidence grew because as my self-defense skills had begun to develop, I was no longer afraid of physical altercations, and this newfound confidence bled into my business life as well. But despite the massive progress I had made in both my fighting skills as well as my mental strength, Takeo constantly talked about the concept of *kaizen*.

Kaizen is a Japanese-originated term that means *continuous improvement* and has been applied to business practices, specifically in the area of standardizing operations. The idea is to evergreen efforts in the areas of efficiency by eliminating wasted efforts in inconsequential areas, and to recalibrate inefficient methods. This commitment to constantly improve was what *kaizen* was all about. One evening, Takeo went into great detail, breaking down the different levels of *kaizen* as we stretched before our workout.

"There are several different phases of *kaizen*. The first is *point kaizen*, which happens very quickly and can be implemented immediately. As soon as any inefficiency is detected, it's immediately corrected, just like correcting your jab so you don't telegraph your punches. Then we have *plane kaizen*. This is the concept of finding ways to scale efficiencies by applying them to other areas, multiplying the benefit. For example, if we discover a more efficient way to strike your jab, there may be kinesthetic elements that can be applied to your hooks and uppercuts. And then we have *cube kaizen*. This is where we can connect the dots and get everything working together in synchronicity. You can have a great jab and a great uppercut, but to become a great fighter, you need to put together the right combinations of punches and slips," Takeo explained.

"So once I have the skills, how do I put them together in a real fight? How will I know what to do?" I asked.

"You have to develop that instinct over time. That's why repetition of the basics is so important. In order to unconsciously react based on instinct, your mind must be void of any distracting thoughts. In martial arts, we call this mental state *mushin*. *Mushin* is the shortened version of *mushin no shin*, which translated to English means *the mind without mind*. What this means is that your mind is void of all distracting thoughts or emotions. When you have less to think about, you can focus more on what's truly important," Takeo philosophized.

This *elimination of the unnecessary* was something that even influenced Takeo's wardrobe. He had two *uniforms*. Uniform number one was his business wardrobe. Black single-breasted suit with a wide peak lapel. Black tie. Crisp white French cuffed shirt. He owned ten sets of this uniform – ten business days of attire. Uniform number two was his social wardrobe. Black t-shirt or black sweater, paired with black stretch denim jeans or black linen drawstring pants. Takeo told me that this minimalist wardrobe eliminated the need to think about what he was going to wear each day. Eliminating extraneous things to think about allowed his mind to focus solely on what it did best, which was creating brilliant business strategies. Minimalizing his wardrobe was one of a seemingly infinite number of strategies Takeo applied to every area of his life, moving him deeper and deeper into a constant state of *mushin*.

This elimination of *all things unnecessary* was the definition of *minimalism*. I always thought of minimalism in terms of aesthetic design, but Takeo taught me that it was more than just an architectural aesthetic or a fashion philosophy. It was an entire philosophy applied to every area of this man's life – a very disciplined way of approaching life.

He explained to me, "Miyamoto Musashi said *'Do nothing which is of no use.'* This means that our focus and our actions must be rooted in precise, intentional, and efficient execution. To do one thing is to not do another. If you're spending time thinking about your woes, you're taking away focus from what you must do. Your entire focus must be on rebuilding now, which involves strengthening your core, because once your core is strong – mentally, emotionally, physically, and spiritually – you'll be able to overcome yourself, and once you overcome yourself, you can overcome anything life throws at you. Okay, let's begin our punch sequence again."

"One."

Pop.

"One, two."

Pop, pop.

"You can only fight the way you practice. One thousand days of lessons for discipline; ten thousand days of lessons for mastery," Takeo would say, quoting Musashi.

I needed to achieve a *mind without mind.* Takeo told me that once I achieved this state of *mushin,* the external world would begin to move in slow motion, and I would be incomparably quicker, nimbler, and sharper. The more time I spent with Takeo, the more I began to connect all the dots and authentically embrace my financial hardship as the most necessary dot in my journey.

As my fighting skills progressed, Takeo began teaching me more complex punch combinations. After my left jab, he taught me to slip to the right and rip a right hook to the body, then explode a right uppercut under the jaw. This punch sequence came right out of Cus D'Amato's boxing playbook, a deadly combination he taught Mike Tyson. This was known as the *six-four* – right hook to the body, to right uppercut. I practiced this sequence over and over, committing myself to mastery.

This sequence became analogous to my new business game plan. In business, I was throwing my jabs and right crosses, but now it was now time to slip to the right and rip my right hook to the body, setting up my jaw-crushing uppercut.

I can't explain how I figured this out, but one night while doing my meditation, it came to me – the exact sequence of plays I needed to execute to rebuild my company. This was undoubtedly a bi-product of finally achieving a state of *mushin*. That evening, I stayed up until three o'clock in the morning, mapping out each step as I saw them in my mind's eye. It was like some sort of divine inspiration as the words magically appeared on my laptop's screen while my fingers moved across the keyboard with the speed and swiftness of a master pianist. I shared everything with Valentina, Isabella, and Takeo of course, and once I had everyone on board with me, I was ready to begin executing my masterpiece.

Most importantly, I knew I had the three most important qualities I needed within my inner circle:

Chūgi, Chūgi, Chūgi.

Loyalty, Loyalty, Loyalty.

Chapter 16
Loyalty, Loyalty, Loyalty

My new goal was no longer to rebuild an office full of *mini-Vincents* like I once had. Instead, I had a two-step plan. Step one was to only go after a very small handful of ex-clients – the largest ones we once had – and handle them myself. Step two was to convince them to introduce me to relationships they had with large institutions. I focused on two types of institutional money management opportunities: municipality pensions and university endowments.

Valentina accompanied me on dozens of business dinners, winning over the wife, hoping the conversation in the car ride home from the restaurant would result in the husband deciding to re-engage in business with me. Similar to what Isabella was to The Icon, Valentina was *my* secret weapon. I truly believe that many of our key relationships were repaired solely due to Valentina's trust-building skills. This was my *six* punch – my right hook to the body.

Valentina and I took the red-eye out of LAX to JFK each Sunday evening, then returned on the last flight back to LAX on each Wednesday afternoon. I spent each Thursday and Friday in our Beverly Hills office. Yes, it was hard on my family, but we all collectively agreed that this was the only way to rebuild.

Isabella stepped up to help too. She understood what this battle entailed, for she had fought a similar battle assisting her husband, The Icon. She encouraged Valentina to hop back into the trenches with me while she took care of Cortez when we traveled to the East Coast.

In many ways, this crazy schedule made our family bonds even tighter. Cortez got to spend more one-on-one time with his grandma, Valentina and I got to spend more one-on-one time together as husband and wife, and when our family reunited together at the end of each week, it felt like a special occasion. What initially felt like a sacrifice and a hardship ended up being a blessing because every internal relationship within our family became stronger.

Valentina was so incredible at connecting with our business associates, as her ability to create meaningful relationships was one of mastery. Dinner after dinner, one by one, slowly but surely, we started to gain momentum without even hiring any new advisors at the firm. This was an entirely new business model.

We fired all the selfish employees and kept the ones that were loyal and willing to fight this war with us, one battle at a time. I remembered The Icon's *Rule #8: Your Beginning Days Of Struggle Will One Day Be Your Good Ole Days*, and we certainly struggled during that time, but Valentina never showed any signs of jet lag or fatigue. I know that our crazy schedule must have pushed her to an insane level of exhaustion, but she never complained once, not one bit. She was an absolute warrior. We relentlessly pursued a small targeted group of ex-clients for the first six months. Of the twelve clients we targeted, we regained nine of them, and due to *The Valentina Effect*, those nine key relationships spread the word to their uber-wealthy friends and made introductions to the institutions they had close relationships with.

After the first year of us implementing our new business model, I was managing three private universities' endowment funds and two cities' pension funds. The gross revenue of our New York office was now about 120% of what it was before the betrayal, just from these nine individual clients and five institutional clients alone. But equally as important, our overhead was only 30% of what it was before the transformation.

We downsized our New York office from 18,000 square feet down to only 3,100 square feet. Prior to the betrayal, we had over one hundred and twenty employees, and now we only had thirteen. Even with a much smaller operation, our net profits were up almost quadruple what they were pre-exodus. I was now making more money than I had ever made, operating out of a much smaller space with a much smaller crew, and I was actually enjoying the people that worked for us. That was the first time in my career I could honestly say that. No more backstabbers. No more greedy advisors grinding me for higher commission splits. No more quitters.

The lack of negative energy created an environment where my people could be more productive. This leaner business model made everyone better – not just happier, but better. The positive energy was contagious, and when a group of like-minded, unselfish, team players get together and operate harmoniously, they can create synergistic momentum.

When our Beverly Hills office's lease came up, we implemented *plane kaizen* – multiplying and scaling the efficiencies of our newly recalibrated New York operation – by implementing these superior principles in our West Coast operation.

I once heard a very successful entrepreneur say that he only employs people that he would enjoy having dinner with – in his home, with his family. When I first heard this, it sounded like a luxury that I would never be able to afford to do. But the more I came to understand this principle – analogous to Takeo and Maria pruning their lime tree – I came to realize that making these decisions was less about fearing potential loss, and more about understanding the potential gain by getting rid of the fungus. Just as I suspected, this implementation of *plane kaizen* in our Beverly Hills office proofed positive as well. We took our drastically increased profit margins and finally began paying down our corporate debt, chipping away at the albatross that hung around my neck for the last two years.

Whenever I shared this good news with Takeo, he was so happy for me. The lessons he taught me were undoubtedly starting to pay off, and I had an entirely new outlook on the war I was fighting. But more importantly, I had an entirely new perception of myself. For the first time in my life, I felt free – free from judgement and free from the burden of feeling like I had to measure up to an impossible level of perfection. I was no longer weighed down by the weight of negative people, and I finally started to soar.

Through this tumultuous time in my life, I learned that the war I had been fighting was not a financial one, nor was it a personal war against Kane and Andrei either. The war I had been fighting my entire life was the war against myself – the emasculating fear that once people found out about all of my flaws, they would all leave me. So many of my life experiences taught me this lie, but what once made me feel like a failure now empowered me. It made me realize that I no longer needed an army of people chanting my name. Just as Zara reminded Takeo, I didn't need *everybody*. I only needed the *right* people, and I only needed a few. The right people in your life will help you repair what is broken, celebrating the battle scars you have collected along the way. Perhaps that was why I fell so deeply in love with the art of *kintsugi*.

Every morning I would wake up and instead of having my signature drink – Americano, two raw sugars, and a dash of cream – I started drinking Japanese matcha tea out of the same *kintsugi* teacup Takeo repaired in his warehouse in Long Beach when we first met. Each time I sipped my tea from that repaired teacup, I thought about that first day Francisco introduced me to Takeo – an introduction that would ultimately save my life. It was a daily reminder that beauty is not about being *perfect*. *True beauty* is rooted in accentuating that which you have *repaired*.

Restoration is about attempting to make what is broken appear perfect, hiding the damage. However *repair* is about taking something broken and improving it, making it even stronger and more beautiful than it was before the initial damage was done, but most importantly, not hiding the damage. Highlighting the damage and accentuating the beauty of its newly repaired state was a different kind of beauty – a more transparent kind of beauty that was far more authentic and far more beautiful.

We were far from a full financial recovery, but at least we were able to start paying down our debt, and with our reduced overhead and increased revenue, it allowed me to breathe. For the first time in three years, I could actually *breathe*. Sure I still had a mountain of debt to pay off, but we were on the rise once again.

Takeo and Maria invited all of us to dinner at their friend's restaurant to celebrate – Isabella, Valentina, Cortez, and me. It was a small, obscure place in Santa Ana – *Ariana Moderna* – named after the chef's daughter.

When we arrived at the address, there was no signage anywhere on the front of the old historic brick building. The rustic exterior of the building was definitely repaired, not restored. It was two stories tall, built in 1929, and with no signage, it was kind of non-descript. I was certain this was the right address, so we parked on the street and walked through the front door, entering a small reception area. The walls were exposed brick with up-lighting embedded in the polished concrete floors that illuminated the 91-year-old bricks, showcasing their historic age and beauty.

"You must be the Montgomery family. Please follow me downstairs," the young, attractive hostess said.

We followed her down a dark, mysterious staircase that led to a basement area that housed a beautiful wine cellar, along with three very special private dining rooms. The vintage Australian cypress wood floor was refinished and highly polished in a rich caramel and honey colored tone, while it maintained its distressed and patinaed qualities. As we entered one of the private dining rooms, we marveled at the dining table as a work of art. Its round tabletop was made of a single slab of translucent white onyx, illuminated from beneath, providing glowing ambient lighting for our intimate room. Takeo and Maria stood up to greet us, as the chef came in to greet us as well.

"This is our dear friend Chef Daniel. He's the master of this unique cuisine we're going to enjoy tonight. Daniel is from Acapulco, but he's also a French-trained chef, so his food is a hybrid of both backgrounds, and it is absolutely spectacular. You're in for a real treat tonight. In fact this year, Daniel earned a Michelin nomination. We're very proud of him," Takeo announced.

Daniel was such a gracious host, and I could tell that this friendship was not just one of restauranteur to patron.

Daniel explained, "I was working in a very famous restaurant in Newport Beach, plus I was doing my own pop-up events here and there back when I first met Takeo and Maria. They were guests of one of my clients that booked a small group event. Maria asked me all kinds of questions about my techniques and my sauces. She eventually hired me to cater several events at their home, and over time, we became friends. A few years later, Takeo invested in me to start *Ariana Moderna*, and he brought all of his big clients here. Once we were running in the black, he handed over the entire restaurant to me. He would never tell you that, but it's true. The Michelin nomination is an honor, but it wouldn't be possible if it weren't for Maria and Takeo."

"No, no, no. Vincent, I need Daniel more than he needs me. You wouldn't believe how many clients I've won over by bringing them here to experience Daniel's food. It is unparalleled. This was just as much an investment in my own business as it was to get Daniel off the ground. My firm has made a lot of money because of what this man creates in this kitchen here," Takeo said.

Daniel shook his head laughing.

"Vincent, Takeo bought this building without even telling me. He put up all the money to get me started, brought in all of our customers, and then gave me all the control and ownership back. He still owns the building, but he doesn't even charge me rent. I argued with him for months over this, but Takeo is not someone you want to argue with," Daniel said laughing, pretending to chop my head off with his imaginary samurai sword.

"Oh, come on Daniel. I just knew your talent was too great for you not to have full control of your artistry. Vincent, Daniel's reservations are now booked out six to seven months in advance," Takeo said.

"So how did we…"

I stopped myself before I asked the question. Daniel smiled. He knew what I was going to ask.

"Anything for Takeo and Maria," Daniel said, deeply bowing to them in reverence.

After the first course came out, I knew we were in for something special. We started off with a *little gem salad* tossed in a unique citrus dressing. The tiny little cherry tomatoes were organically grown in Daniel's private rooftop garden and exploded in your mouth with unbelievable flavor. Takeo had a special irrigation system installed on the roof of the building to accommodate Daniel's most strict growing standards. This cruciferous masterpiece was topped with shaved Parmigiano-Reggiano, imported from Modena, Italy. Simple and elegant.

Next was his signature Sinaloan *aguachile de camaron* served individually to each guest in a small *molcajete*. The combination of savory and spicy flavors that accentuated the sweetness of the giant prawns was delightful. The limes, cucumbers, cilantro, and serrano chiles were all organically grown in Daniel's rooftop garden as well, of course.

The third course was grilled octopus, brought in fresh from the Gulf of Mexico, marinated in a tangy citrus sauce with peanuts and cilantro, served with a hand-torn piece of the most amazing rustic French crusty bread. Daniel made all of his bread in-house in a wood burning oven that was also located on the rooftop of the building.

The fourth course was butter-poached lobster served à la carte on a giant white *kintsugi* plate with gold veins running through its bright porcelain opulence.

But the showstopper was something from another world. Daniel's pièce de résistance was his *tacos al carbon*. He only used Japanese waygu beef for this dish. The combination between the decadence and extravagance of $200 per pound waygu beef and the simplicity of a taco was magical. He grilled the waygu on an open flame using a Japanese *hibachi* grill and sourced his mesquite charcoal from a special connection in Nuevo Leon, a sovereign state in the Northeastern region of Mexico where the best mesquite came from.

The secret behind his handmade tortillas was that he sourced his corn from Yaxunah, Mexico. This was the original corn that the ancient Mayans used for over one thousand years to make their tortilla *masa*, completely different than the GMO corn we have here in the states. Daniel traveled to Yaxunah himself to learn the process directly from a Mayan woman whose *Cochinita Pibil* tacos are world-renowned. He had this amazing corn imported from Yaxunah, and they ground their own masa right there in Daniel's kitchen.

These tacos were incredible. The marbleized waygu had a smoky, mesquite aroma unlike anything I had tasted in my life. Both the waygu and the tortilla just melted in your mouth like warm butter. Chef Daniel paired this dish with an amazing red wine called *Portrait* from a small boutique organic winery in Napa Valley.

He explained to us, "This is a 2016 blend. One of my best friends took me to visit this winery in Napa and I spoke to the ambassador of the vineyard. Her name was Brianna and she told me the most inspiring story about this particular vintage. Apparently, Napa Valley went through a pretty rough drought between 2012 and 2016. That's five years in a row of drought. Five years in a row of struggle. You see, when grape vines get plenty of water and plenty of sunshine, they're healthy and grow mostly leaves. They're very verdant and grow like crazy, but the fruit content is watered down. However when there's a drought, it's the opposite. The vines produce far less leaves and far less grapes because they're conserving resources, but they channel all their energy into those fewer grapes. The grapes' content becomes far richer and more concentrated because all of the vine's energy gets focused into those fewer grapes. As a result, what you get are wines that age extremely well, and are far more complex. In fact even in your glass, the wine will literally change as you enjoy it. When you take the first few sips, you'll experience certain impressions, and then additional aromas and flavors gradually emerge as you continue to enjoy it, kind of like watching a flower as it blossoms. This particular wine is a blend – 38% Cabernet Sauvignon, 34% Cabernet Franc, and 28% Merlot – so you get to experience the different textures on your palate, and they all have something different to offer. A great blend creates a harmony and synchronicity between the different varietals."

Daniel instructed us to take a bite of the waygu tacos, and then take sip of the wine. It was a perfect pairing – simple, yet complex. It was analogous to each of Takeo's relationships – *simple* in that his friendships were rooted in the seven tenets of the *Bushidō* code, yet *complex* in how deep and multifaceted his bonds were with his friends. As I thought about his treasured relationships – with his wife and son, with T-Mack, with Zara, with Daniel, and with Rob and Cher Charleston – each relationship was the perfect pairing, just like the waygu tacos and the *Portait* wine.

Daniel continued, "This is Takeo's favorite wine, which makes sense if you understand the soul of this man. The greater the adversity the vine faces, the more concentrated and powerful the grape becomes. The more concentrated and powerful the grape becomes, the more complex and rich the wine becomes. This is the same lesson Takeo has been teaching me about every facet of my life. This particular vintage struggled in drought for the longest period of time – five years in a row – and of all the recent vintages from this vineyard within the last decade, this is the best one according to Takeo's palate."

Every last preference Takeo had – whether art, or jewelry, or wine – was connected to his proclivity towards overcoming tough times. The story of this wine was a metaphor for life. Nothing great ever comes from easy times. It is only out of struggle that greatness is born, and often times, the longer the struggle and the greater the adversity, the more powerful and beautiful the outcome. It was obvious that Takeo was more than just a financier of Daniel's restaurant. He was also a true mentor. As the evening came to an end, Takeo pulled me into the other room. I could tell this was something important.

"Vincent, I have to talk to you about something. I've been watching the markets in Asia, and there's something happening over there. They think it's some sort of virus, and the death toll is increasing at an alarming rate. My gut is telling me something's going to happen on a global scale. It's starting to affect my business because I have wealthy clients in Hong Kong and Seoul, and I think it's going to eventually affect your business too. It's just a matter of time," Takeo said.

"So what does this all mean?" I asked.

"My sources are talking about this thing turning into a pandemic, and if that happens, a lot of businesses are going to get shut down, and the markets are going to start crashing. We need to get out in front of this, and I have a plan. It might even involve us partnering up in some capacity and doing something together. Are you interested in teaming up?" he asked.

"Of course I would. Are you kidding me?" I answered.

"Vincent, if this virus comes over here, it could mean the collapse of the entire financial services world. It will be worse than

2008, and possibly worse than *The Great Depression*. But I have a plan," Takeo said.

"What's the plan?" I eagerly asked.

"Let's meet tomorrow and discuss what I have in mind. In fact, I have a meeting in Century City tomorrow afternoon. I'll stop by your house after I wrap up, probably around seven-ish," Takeo said.

Takeo was a calculated man, and he wouldn't have taken this so seriously if he didn't know something. He built an unbelievably successful company by innovating – skating to where the puck was going while everyone else hovered around where the puck had been – and if anyone had a pulse on what was to come, it was Takeo.

Chapter 17
Behind Bars

Takeo was adamant that the virus circulating in Asia would make its way to America. When he talked about it, it sounded like something out of a science fiction movie – completely unrealistic – yet I trusted his judgement. He had a special talent of gathering and synthesizing information from unconventional sources, then figuring out how the dots would connect in the future.

In addition to Takeo's primary business, he also had his own hedge fund – something he had been beta testing with his own money for several years. He said it was more of a hobby than a business. At least that's how he described it.

To call a $100 million hedge fund a *hobby* was hilarious, yet it was a very *Takeo* thing to say. He allowed a very small group of friends to participate in his fund, but that only comprised $29 million of its assets. The other $71 million was Takeo's own capital. He fully believed that the storm was coming and was prepared to bet heavily on his intuition. I explained to both Valentina and Isabella everything that Takeo explained to me. I fully expected them to be resistant to this ridiculously paranoid theory, but they listened intently.

Isabella said, "Vincent, I have some very good friends in Shanghai and Hong Kong that have been telling me stories very similar to what Takeo has been telling you. I also have friends in Milan, Italy that have told me similar stories. I too think something very bad is going to happen. I can't explain it, but I can feel it in my bones."

Isabella had always been an adept investor, and though many assumed her ex-supermodel status was merely about her physical beauty, she developed several powerful international connections during her modeling days. She became a student of the Asian and European financial markets when she wasn't sashaying down runways in Paris and Milan. While all the other runway models were out partying, she used her modeling career as her foot in the door to meet important people she could learn investment strategies from. Part of the reason The Icon's wealth grew exponentially was due to investing his business profits in investment opportunities that were made accessible through Isabella's connections. They were a great team in so many ways.

"So what exactly is Takeo proposing?" Valentina asked.

"He's reallocated all of his positions in his hedge fund based on this global phenomenon. He invested in top multi-brand online retailers because he thinks a pandemic will shut down conventional brick-and-mortar retail shopping as we know it. This would cause a surge in electronic payments, so he's invested in companies that provide these services as well. Plus, if people are locked up at home in quarantine, companies with video conferencing services will soar. Takeo is expecting some of these stocks to produce up to 78% returns in less than a year," I explained.

"This sounds like crazy talk," Valentina replied, and just as my overly-sensitive defensive self was about to start an argument, Valentina said, "But Vincent, if this is something you really believe in, I'm with you 100%."

Isabella told me, "My husband didn't become this successful by playing it safe in life. He too had the impeccable ability to follow his hunches in a thoroughly calculated manner, different than Takeo, but similar. Can you set up a meeting with Takeo here at the house? I'd really like to talk to him about this."

"Of course. He's actually coming over around seven o'clock tonight to meet with me. Would you like to talk to him then?" I asked.

"That would be great," Isabella confirmed.

When Takeo arrived at our house, we sat around the main center island in the kitchen. Isabella shared stories of what her overseas friends had told her about their experiences, and Takeo shared what his research had been telling him. I knew Isabella was a business-savvy woman, but hearing her carry on this conversation with Takeo was like sitting in a boardroom with The Icon himself. She was polished, yet approachable; sharp, yet graceful; and inquisitive without being interrogative.

After an hour of conversation, Isabella asked all of us, "Would you mind if I spoke with Takeo privately for a moment?"

"Of course. Valentina, let's go out back by the pool. You guys can come outside and join us when you're done," I said.

As Valentina and I sat under the palapa-covered pavilion by the pool, Isabella and Takeo moved into the living room to continue their conversation.

"What do you think they're talking about?" I asked Valentina.

"I have no idea, but you know how much mama loves you. She's one of your fiercest protectors. She's probably vetting Takeo for you," she said.

I remember The Icon telling me that over 90% of everything great in his life was because of Isabella. Though I thought I understood what he meant, witnessing her conversation with Takeo that night made me realize that The Icon wasn't just talking about their family life and their social life. He was talking about their success in business as well.

Valentina continued, "Most people think mama merely did the schmoozing with the wives of Papa's business associates, but she was also reading and vetting those businessmen too. She was just as instrumental in making business decisions as Papa was."

"Kind of like you and me," I said.

Valentina smiled and slightly blushed, looking down towards the flagstone pool deck, modestly nodding in agreement.

Just then, Isabella and Takeo walked outside to join us. Isabella had a mischievous grin on her face, almost identical to Valentina's signature expression when she had an unconventional idea.

"Takeo and I have been talking about what we think the markets are going to do over the next six to nine months, and he's graciously opened his hedge fund to me. He's agreed to take in new money from you too. I'm going to move $400 million over to Takeo's fund, and I'm going to suggest you move some of your money over too. It's obviously up to you, but I really believe in Takeo's vision on this one," Isabella said.

"Look guys, I'm happy to let you participate in this, but as you know, with any investment, this comes with its fair share of risk. This fund is purely based on my intuition, and if it doesn't work out, I don't want this to affect our friendship. I just moved over some more of my own capital into this fund, and I have a very small group of friends that are going in big with me. If you're worried about doing this at all, as your friend, I'm going to tell not to do it. Now, I normally charge two-and-twenty, but for you guys, I won't charge anything," Takeo said.

Two-and-twenty was pretty standard for hedge funds. It meant that the hedge fund manager would charge a 2.00% fee on the liquid assets they managed for you, plus another 20% on any gains they produced for you above a benchmark. Takeo was basically offering to work for free, and if his predictions were right, he would have no upside on our money whatsoever. He was only letting us into his fund as a favor.

Though Isabella moving over $400 million sounded like a big number, that was only 10% of her total liquid net worth. Isabella didn't need to incur any financial risk at this point in her life. It would be almost impossible for her to ever run out of money, but she explained, "I'm already playing it ultra-conservative. If the market crashes, I'll be just fine, so I'm not doing this because of fear. I'm doing this because I think it's exciting, but for you kids, this is the kind of move that could elevate you to a whole different level."

Takeo once told me about some friends of his – a successful elderly couple. The husband was in advertising, and the wife was an ex-professional tennis player. They did well for themselves, but in the 1970's, they started collecting contemporary art. It was the right time, they were in the right place, and they met the right people. They bought one painting for $25,000 and later sold it for $300,000. Then they used that $300,000 to buy another painting – a *Basquiat* – and later sold it for $11 million. Today, they have a collection worth over $70 million. That *Basquiat* transaction was what put them in a completely different league, and from there, they parlayed that transaction and grew their wealth exponentially. I desperately wanted Takeo's fund to be my *Basquiat*, but I didn't have the money to invest. I still had over $23 million of corporate debt to pay off. Valentina looked at me with that same mischievous grin Isabella had when she approached us.

I ashamedly confessed, "Okay. You all know what I've been through and what my current financial situation is. If this is the right move – which I believe it is – I feel like I'm missing out because I just don't have the money to invest at the moment."

"What are you talking about? We have $35 million to move over from our *Madre's Coffee* money," Valentina said.

I interjected, "No, YOU have $35 million to move, and I think you should. But that's…"

"Vincent, stop it! We already talked about this. It's OUR money, not MINE," Valentina strongly stated.

Isabella walked up to me and gently placed her warm hands on my trembling cheeks, looking into my eyes with a depth of love that had no limits.

Isabella softly said, "Sweetheart. I know what you're saying and I understand what you're feeling. Papa never told you this, but when he went through that turmoil with Joan Gastineau, *The Hotel 100* was running in the red – deep in the red. He poured everything he had into that hotel and when things started to crumble, he was very hard on himself – too hard on himself. At that point, we were engaged and I was still modeling full-time. I had just finished doing a big cosmetic campaign, so I had a few hundred thousand coming in from that job, and I had another $1.8 million in savings. Even though we weren't married yet, I gave him everything I had. I even sold my engagement ring without him knowing. He needed every last dime we had to keep the business afloat."

I couldn't believe my ears. I had never heard this story, and neither had Valentina.

"We got married on the beach, just the two of us, Francisco, Miguel, Jorge, and Flor – no other guests – just our pastor and our family. I got my dress from a little boutique in Santa Monica. It was a simple, white crocheted dress that only cost forty dollars. Right after we got married, I quit my modeling career because I knew he needed my help to rebuild what Joan had sabotaged, and we spent that next year rebuilding his key business relationships. We were taking people to dinner almost every night, repairing his reputation. He was so thankful that I was willing to do that, but he felt awful about it. I made him swear to never tell anyone what I had done," Isabella explained.

"Why did you want to keep that a secret?" Valentina asked.

"Because Papa was a *man* and I thought it would be better for him if I protected his male ego. That's what a woman is supposed to do for her man if she really believes in him. I never wanted any credit for it. I just knew he needed me to go all-in with him, so that's what I did," said Isabella.

"So what happened when Papa found out about your ring?" Valentina asked.

"He was so upset with me and he was adamant about replacing it, so I let him buy me a temporary, simple, white gold wedding band – the one I'm wearing now. I'm not the type of woman that needs to walk around flaunting an enormous diamond ring. I don't need to impress other people with flashy jewelry. Plus, this simple wedding band means something special to me. It represents what our marriage was always about – commitment, not possessions. It's kind of funny how the *temporary* ring became my *permanent* ring, as well as my *favorite* ring. It reminds me of our *Good Ole Days*. In retrospect, I think I may have done you a disservice by not sharing this with you earlier because it's an example of how a wife is supposed to step up for her husband when her husband is in need, and it's also proof that a husband allowing his wife to do that doesn't make him any less of a man," Isabella said.

In my book *The Icon Effect*, I wrote about the *24 Rules* The Icon had taught me. Rule #6 was *Accepting Help Doesn't Make You Any Less Of A Man*. When I was first getting to know The Icon, I wondered why this man was being so generous towards me, at first with this time, and then with his money. This concept of going all-in with someone was something that all of us *Icon beneficiaries* experienced first-hand. But as the layers of the onion were slowly peeled back, the first person to really set this powerful ripple effect in motion was Isabella. In her marriage, there was no *mine* versus *yours*. Everything with her and The Icon was *theirs*.

"Vincent, you and Valentina are a fantastic team. Use the *Madre's Coffee* money to stake you guys in Takeo's fund. Plus, Takeo has something he wants to share with you too, Vincent," said Isabella.

Takeo then said, "I've been thinking a lot about my fund and what it is today. After talking to Isabella, I think I want to start opening it up to more clients – more of the *right* clients. I want to partner up with you on a segregated fund inside my fund. We would be partners – 50/50. I think we could make a great team. What do you think about this?"

I looked at Isabella, and then Valentina. They were both so excited for me. They knew I needed a big win, and they also knew how much I admired Takeo. I looked at him through my glassy eyes and nodded my head, smiling while attempting to hold back tears, and said, "It would be an honor to partner with you Takeo. Thank you for believing in me," followed by a deep bow – the kind of bow a student gives his sensei.

I still remember watching the news on television as the virus spread throughout Asia. It looked like a complete hoax at first, but as time unraveled, more and more people became infected and ended up in the hospital on ventilators – so many in fact that the hospitals were running out of capacity. It was surreal, like watching a movie. We were outside spectators in the states, and like most Americans, I thought this was something that would only happen to *other* people.

Takeo and I started taking in new money from investors and in a very short amount of time, we were managing just over $3 billion in assets.

Then the unimaginable happened. Our local and federal government declared the virus a national pandemic and instituted a mandatory quarantine. Nobody could even leave their house except to go to the grocery store. It was like we were all locked up, living behind bars. I figured we'd be quarantined for a week, which seemed like a long time, but this was just the beginning.

The first week went by, then the second, then the third. Restaurants and bars shut down completely. An entire month went by with no progress in containing the virus and no vaccine in sight. The stock market did things it had never done before. Oil was trading at negative forty bucks a barrel. Everything was tanking, including our fund.

One of the biggest multi-brand online retailers we invested in was down 12% from the beginning of March until the end of March. In addition, one of the video conferencing services we stacked our chips on opened at 151 on March 28th, but then plummeted down to 113 just seven days later.

"Takeo, are you worried?" I asked.

"Vincent, we're only a few weeks in. The markets are freaking out right now and people are panicking. Everything will be noisy for the first couple of months, but you must quiet your mind. Don't get distracted by the hysteria you see in the news. Our strategy is principle-based, not emotionally-based. We must stay the course," Takeo reassured me.

Takeo had the composure of a Zen master, but I was extremely worried. Isabella's $400 million investment was now only worth $368 million, taking a $32 million loss in just one month. Valentina's $35 million account had lost $2.8 million. Things were not looking good for us.

While Takeo, Valentina, and Isabella remained cool as a popsicle in the freezer, I was melting like an ice cream sandwich on a scorching hot summer day. They all reassured me that one month was not an adequate time frame to judge any investment decisions, but I must admit, taking a hit that big in that short amount of time made me physically nauseous.

I worried that I made the wrong decision to partner with Takeo on this project because if things continued to tank, I would never be able to forgive myself for dragging my family into yet another financial catastrophe. The mere thought of falling deeper and deeper into the abyss was something that made me start to emotionally unravel again. The level of certainty Takeo had in all of his decisions was something I envied. He was 100% principle-driven and never questioned his decisions, regardless of what the scoreboard said.

"Vincent, we're in the top of the third inning. Now is not the time to panic," he said calmly, having lost over $15.2 million of his own money within the last 30 days.

"How can you be so calm about this?" I frantically asked.

Takeo replied, "Remember when Chef Daniel shared how the drought produced the best grapes? Well, a great winemaker has to make difficult decisions every single year, and every year presents a new cocktail of uncertainties. The winemaker that produced that incredible *Portrait* 2016 vintage we enjoyed that evening faced a new challenge the very next year. The drought ended and there was an abundance of rain and sunshine, which created a different quandary for her. It's called *The Goldilocks Zone* – the perfect combination of water and soil type that produces the *best* wine by most sommeliers' standards. That's what happened in 2017 which produced the *1886 Cabernet Sauvignon* in 2018. Personally, I prefer the more concentrated and complex wines that come from distressed conditions, but most sommeliers prefer the easier, smoother finish of the *1886 Cabernet Sauvignon*."

"But that doesn't seem like it had anything to do with the winemaker's skill. Wasn't that just luck? If the weather was perfect, didn't the vines just get what they needed automatically? Where's the skill and expertise in that?" I asked.

Takeo explained, "It's a different kind of skill. The brave decision the winemaker made was to do nothing in 2017 when she believed she was in *The Goldilocks Zone*. You need a great deal of wisdom and discernment to trust in the elements and stay the course during a time like this. You don't change the soil. You don't irrigate. You literally do nothing. The perfect combination of these naturally occurring elements can create an amazing outcome, but you must trust that *The Goldilocks Zone* is real, resisting the urge to change anything in the equation. When you panic and question everything, your emotions want to make changes and adjustments, reacting to every little element. When it's sunny, instead of being thankful for the sun, you worry that there's too much sun. When it rains, instead of being thankful for the rain, you worry that it might be too much water. But when your intuition tells you that you're in *The Goldilocks Zone*, you've got to have the discipline to stay the course and let the outcome unfold organically, and right now, I believe we're in our own financial *Goldilocks Zone*. Stay the course with me on this one Vincent."

The market was so volatile, but the clients we acquired were unbelievably devoted to Takeo. In some ways, their faith in Takeo's vision was even greater than mine, which made me feel guilty for not trusting his discernment more. Our fund showed a mild increase during April, but trickled back into a slow decline in May. I was so worried I had made a terrible decision.

"What have I gotten my family into?" I muttered under my breath as I watched our fund slowly bleed to death.

An 8% loss in the first month was definitely not good, but what concerned me even more was the future. If things didn't improve, I was deathly afraid of what our clients would think about our fund that was built purely on Takeo's speculation. It's one thing to take losses alongside the masses, but when you take heavy losses due to betting on an unconventional idea that someone talked you into, it is far more upsetting.

Isabella could see the guilt and despair in my eyes as I ate breakfast with our family each morning, obsessing over where the market closed the day before. One night after dinner, she said, "Come with me Vincent. Let's take a stroll out back."

As we walked down the pathway to the pavilion by the pool, Isabella gently placed her hand in the crease of my elbow, allowing me to escort her on our stroll and said, "Vincent, I know you're worried. Don't be. We all knew the risks going into Takeo's fund. Yes, we lost some money initially, but it's not the first time I've lost money, and it certainly won't be the last time either. It's all part of being an investor. Most people panic as soon as they take a hit, and they immediately sell off their positions, but as an investor, you must have staying power. You must stand in your positions if you really believe in them, even when you're taking huge losses. We're only down 8% so far."

"Actually, we're down 8.92% as of today," I said, correcting her generous attempt to round down my failure.

"Vincent, don't be so hard on yourself. First of all, we're only a few months in. I only evaluate my positions every six months. Looking at your gains and losses on a daily basis is like stepping on the scale everyday while you're on a diet. You'll drive yourself crazy. Second of all, I can tell you're afraid that I'm going to blame you. Sweetheart, I've lost and gained more money in my investments in one single day than your fund has lost in three months. We'll be just fine, but let me ask you something. Do you still believe in Takeo's vision?"

I took a deep breath attempting to hide my embarrassment from Isabella, and in a slightly trembling voice that quivered with shame, I said, "I do. I just… I just don't… I just don't want to let you down again."

"Again? Sweetheart, what do you mean *again*?" Isabella compassionately asked.

I took another deep breath as I stared down at the ground and embarrassingly admitted, "Your family has given me everything I have. Your husband took me under his wing like I was his own son, entrusting me to run his company, and I failed. I single-handedly destroyed everything The Icon gave me. If it wasn't for Takeo's advice and Valentina's willingness to help me rebuild, I don't think I could have… I don't think… I don't think I could have even made it this far. The thought of losing everything your husband gave me made me want to kill myself. I just hated myself for it. And now, I just lost over $35 million of your money, and over $3 million of Valentina's."

"Vincent, look at me. You have NEVER let me down. Those things that happened to your business – those are things that happen to every successful person's business at some point. We're all hit with adversities in our lives – all of us. It happened to Papa with *The Hotel 100*. It happened to Takeo's firm too. So the fact that it happened to your business shouldn't come as a surprise to you. Every successful businessperson I know has experienced something similar to this – betrayal, personal attacks, financial hardships – these are all part of running a successful business. And don't you dare – even for one second – think that you have let down my husband or his legacy. He would be so proud of you right now, fighting to make your comeback. He always found so much romance in a great comeback, and that's exactly what you're doing right now," Isabella said, encouraging me the way The Icon used to, but in her own special way.

Sometimes we all need reassurance that we are forgiven, but more importantly, that we were never blamed in the first place for things we harbor massive guilt over. It is easy to stop loving ourselves when we feel we are the cause of hurting the ones we love. This burdensome feeling of guilt – albeit misplaced and self-inflicted – is a burden that can only be lifted by a guardian angel. During this time when I seemed damaged beyond repair, Isabella was there to repair my confidence in a way that only a guardian angel could. She was always the master *kintsugi* artisan whose golden epoxy shined the brightest.

"Vincent, Takeo has trained you well. You stay the course with him. With any great business venture – as well as with any great business partnership – you need to go all-in and stay committed to your partner no matter what. If it fails, at least you know you did everything in your power to make it succeed, and the bond of that relationship will be something you will treasure for the rest of your life. But if you jump ship on your partner, that relationship will never be the same," Isabella encouraged.

My shoulders slowly rolled forward as my head sank deeper into my torso, and in a faint voice filled with worry, I asked her, "And if it doesn't succeed?"

"Then you can add it to your collection of battle scars and move on to your next conquest with Takeo as your partner – as your brother. Vincent, this is a partnership you don't want to give up on. Takeo understands your battle scars and embraces them as your mentor, your business partner, and as your friend. You know, my husband hid his battle scars from everyone, and believe me, he had plenty. In fact, it was his scars that made him so beautiful, but he ever really saw it that way. He was a great man – the greatest man I have ever known – but the one area of his life I never agreed with was that he hid his challenges from the ones he loved. I understand

and admire why he did it, but I believe doing so robs the people around you of appreciating who you really are. Part of the way God brings people together is by creating opportunities for us to step up for one another. This is how true love is realized – when you're in the foxhole together and your partner is fighting side-by-side with you. This is when you find out what kind of relationship you truly have," Isabella said.

"But I feel like I've been such a burden to Valentina. She's been so amazing, and I hate the fact that I've put her through all of this. I hate myself for it," I embarrassingly admitted.

"Vincent, what makes you a great man is your authenticity. That's one of the main reasons Valentina fell in love with you in the first place. She trusts you 100% because you tell her everything and she knows she can trust you. You allow her to participate in every element of your life – the good, the bad, and the ugly – and that gives her the opportunity to step up for you. That's a real gift you have given her. You may feel like you've burdened her, but it's just the opposite. You've gifted her the opportunity to express her love for you. This is one of your best qualities that we all love about you. Joseph used to tell me stories about you in this regard, and Francisco still tells me that he marvels at how transparent you are with people. But of all your fans – and yes, Joseph and Francisco have always been your fans – Valentina is by far your biggest fan and greatest admirer. She says you are the most fearless man she has ever met. And do you know why? It's because you hide nothing. You aren't afraid to let people see your imperfections, and you hide your true feelings from no one. This is your power Vincent – your willingness to hide your scars from no one and continue to fight relentlessly. You're on the rise right now. You may not see it, but I see it, and so does Valentina. It's time for you to start believing in yourself again. You need to go all-in with Takeo, but more importantly, you need to go all-in with yourself," Isabella said.

The *Vincent* of the past would not have been able to accept Isabella's words because I would not have been able to forgive myself, but due to the *Isabella Effect* and the *Valentina Effect*, this new *Vincent 2.0* was *kintsugi-repaired*.

Isabella then said the most empowering thing anyone has ever said to me.

"Vincent, they say the bird perched on the branch has no fear of the branch breaking beneath it because its faith isn't rooted in the *branch*. Its faith is rooted in its *wings*. Sweetheart, you've built up strong wings over the years because you've had so many branches break beneath you, and yet you've always been able to fly to a new branch. You had the fortitude to rebuild your company, completely changing your business model in the midst of almost losing everything. Not many people would have been able to do what you've done. You should be proud of yourself. Don't worry about the branch breaking beneath you. You have strong wings, and I know you will soar with Takeo."

I cannot logically or scientifically prove this, but the power of believing in yourself seems to communicate to the universe that it is *your* time. You can have every other element in place – the right business, the right business partner, God's grace, and even be in *The Goldilocks Zone* – but if you don't believe in yourself, you have nothing. Perhaps that was why The Icon always appeared so confident, because he knew his wings were strong.

The more Isabella shared with me the challenges my mentor experienced, the more I realized the source of his confidence didn't come from what he had achieved, but rather what he had overcome. That was what made his wings so strong. I could easily say the same thing about Takeo. This realization allowed me to forgive myself for all the mistakes I had made, take pride in what I had overcome, and start believing in myself again. I allowed myself to embrace my volatile path, and just like that, the very next month, Takeo's intuition began to proof positive.

When the market closed on June 1st, Takeo's fund was up 81% since early April. By August 1st, it was up 137%. Then another month went by. Then another. This was an unprecedented time. Some industries completely shut down forever while new ones popped up to facilitate a *new normal* environment.

By October – the sixth month of our country being locked up at home – Takeo's fund was up 451%. Takeo had turned Valentina's $35 million into over $192 million in seven months.

We used some of it to completely payoff 100% of the firm's debt, and still had an insane amount left over. But what made me the happiest was that Takeo had turned Isabella's $400 million into $2.2 billion. It was her idea to not only invest in Takeo's vision, but also to propose that he and I formally get into business together. This could have only been orchestrated by my guardian angel.

Our fund's reputation started to spread exponentially, and our clients' friends were begging us to let them into our fund. We set a minimum of $100 million of liquid investable assets per client to get in. The same clients I was scraping to hold on to when Andrei and Kane pillaged my client roster were now calling me, begging to get into our fund, and we turned them all down because their $25 million of investable assets was just too small for us now. I must admit, it felt good to reject clients that had rejected me back when I was struggling to stay afloat.

My *kintsugi* gold was now shining brightly, my lime tree was rid of its fungus, and I was delivering my *six-four punch combination* like a master.

There was certainly a time when my darkest days were so dark, I doubted whether the sun would ever rise again, but as Takeo always told me, this was all just part of the cycle.

Chapter 18
The Cycle

The most important things in my life were never things that I did anything to *deserve*. I did not *earn* them. My wife, my son, and my mentors were all *given* to me as gifts – as true blessings.

My chance encounter with one man in a coffee shop – The Icon – led me to Francisco, Joseph, Isabella, and ultimately to Valentina. But as much gratitude as I had for these amazing relationships, I realized that I must also be grateful for my experience with Andrei and Kane. Had I not suffered their betrayal, Francisco would not have introduced me to Takeo. This experience that felt like a death blow was the very thing that enriched my life and helped me discover who I really wanted to be. Life has a funny way of closing certain doors so that new alternative doors can open for us.

As Musashi Miyamoto wrote in his *Dokkōdō* 獨行道 one week before his death, "Never let yourself be saddened by a separation."

When people betray us and extricate themselves from our lives, it should never bring upon depression or sadness. These separations are actually blessings in disguise. Each time I thought about the so-called coincidental chain of events that shaped my life, it posed so many *what if* questions.

What if I had never met The Icon?

What if The Icon had never introduced me to Francisco?

And what if Francisco had never introduced me to Takeo?

Every time I thought about these questions, my eyes would well up with tears of gratitude. My relationship with The Icon was an example of how the right mentor can change the course of your life, forever. This was the definition of *The Icon Effect*.

I arranged a dinner at *Amor*, the same restaurant where I proposed to Valentina, in the same private dining room – *The*

Primero Room. Valentina and I invited Takeo and Maria, Francisco and his wife Santana, and Isabella of course.

That room brought back so many great memories. As we entered the room, our table had nine place settings, but there were only seven of us. Our server asked if I wanted the remaining two place settings removed, but I quietly informed him that there would be two last guests joining us that evening.

"I would like to propose a toast," I said standing up as our server brought in eight flutes of *Siete Leguas* blanco tequila and one single flute of sparkling apple cider.

"Takeo, when The Icon and Joseph passed away, I was lost. They were my mentors – they were my best friends. After Andrei and Kane betrayed me, I had completely lost my faith in people, and most importantly, I temporarily lost my faith in God. But then you came along and taught me things that I desperately needed to learn – things that only you could have taught me," I announced.

My voice became filled with intense emotion and my breath became heavy, matching the heaviness of my heart. I looked around the room, soaking in this precious moment just as Valentina had taught me to do.

"Thank you Takeo. You saved my life. You..."

I couldn't utter another word. Only Takeo and I understood what I meant by that. He and I were the only people in that room that had considered taking our own lives in our darkest moments when we were lost in the abyss, yet someone pulled us out. For me, it was Takeo. For Takeo, it was Rob Charleston. It was a secret that we would take to our graves with us. In both of our marriages, there were no secrets except for this one, and the bond that these horrific times in our lives created between the two of us was unbreakable. I struggled to continue my toast, but I regained my composure.

"And so in honor of Takeo, I have two surprises this evening. The first is a small gift," I said as I had one of our servers bring it into the room.

It was a long Manzanita branch – about seven feet long. When displayed horizontally on a wall as an art installation, the branch started on an upward trajectory from left to right, hitting a peak halfway through. At its peak was a knot in the branch. Then the branch took a steep downwards turn, and at its trough was another knot, just before the branch drastically began to curve upwards again, ending with its tip far higher than the previous peak at the branch's midpoint.

"Takeo, this branch tells the story of everything you have taught me about life. First, Manzanitas can live in places with very poor soil quality and very little water. They are extremely drought tolerant. Similar to what Daniel shared with us at his restaurant about the drought the *Portrait* wine vines endured, this particular Manzanita species has the ability to bear the unbearable, which is what you taught me how to do," I explained.

Takeo was fascinated, as he was so passionate about artistic symbolism.

I continued, "In addition, the shape of this branch tells us the story of life and success. As the branch begins its upward trajectory, it represents the illusion that success is linear, and that success will continue that linear path upwards. The knot at the peak symbolizes the beginning of life's second act, and as the branch begins to curve downward, this symbolizes a major downfall – similar to when both of our businesses were destroyed. As the branch curves downwards, we see we it hit a trough – the low point – and we see another knot in the branch at that low point. That knot is where we decide how we will define our faith. That's the moment where we have to believe that the sun will rise again. This is when Francisco introduced me to you – at my low point. The branch then dramatically curves upward, with its tip ending in a much higher position than its previous peak, symbolic of what you did for me," I said as my voice trembled with emotion.

Even Takeo's eyes became glassy as I explained the story of the Manzanita branch to him, for it was more than just a piece of art. It was more than just a Manzanita branch. It symbolized his life's work – his life's journey – his legacy.

I continued, "And lastly, this branch symbolizes something very special that Isabella taught me. '*The bird perched on the branch does not fear the branch breaking beneath it because its faith is not rooted in the branch. Its faith is rooted in the strength of its wings.'* This branch – this symbol of success – can break at any time, but my wings are stronger than ever because of everything you taught me. You once shared with me the scripture, *'No greater love hath a man than he lay down his life for his friend.'* That's what you did for me."

Takeo's bottom lip started to quiver as he walked over to me, bowing deeply, followed by an extra-long embrace.

"What gallery did you find such an exquisite piece of art, Vincent?" Takeo asked me.

I smiled. During one of my darkest hours, I drove up to the mountains in Idyllwild to meditate as I tried to figure out a solution to my then financial challenges. On that day trip, I took my athletic gear with me and did an intense Tabata session – perhaps the most intense session I had ever done. It was such an emotionally-charged workout, I couldn't tell where the tears running down my face started and the sweat dripping down my face ended.

As I descended down the mountain following my Tabata climb, I asked God for a sign – a sign that my life was worth living – a sign to let me know that He had not forsaken me. And in the midst of that prayer, I saw the branch. It was laying sideways, just as I presented it to Takeo, right in the middle of the trail. I don't remember seeing it there during my ascension up the trail. In fact I'm certain it was not there on my way up. I would have had to jump over it on my climb up the trail.

In the midst of our most troubled times when our spirit cries out to God in exhaustive desperation, I believe on rare occasions, God gives us signs to let us know that He is still walking with us, encouraging us to continue to walk with Him.

This branch was one of those signs.

I picked up that branch, placed it in my car, and cried the entire drive home back to Los Angeles that afternoon. It was at that moment I knew He was still with me. That was the day after Isabella shared with me the story about the bird perched on the branch. I took that Manzanita branch home and peeled off the dead bark and sanded it down with 400-grit sandpaper, then drilled two small holes in the back of the branch so that it could be mounted on a wall with two simple finishing nails. At first I thought I would hang it on the wall in the living room of my man cave, but after seeing everything unfold in spectacular fashion, I knew this should belong to Takeo. I knew he would appreciate this gift more than any expensive luxury item I could buy him. That branch embodied everything Takeo had given me.

"I also have a second surprise for you Takeo. I have invited two very special guests. Hold on one moment," I said, excusing myself from the table and from *The Primero Room*.

When I returned just a few seconds later, I escorted our two special guests into the room.

"Ladies and gentlemen, I present Rob and Cher Charleston," I announced with great joy.

I had contacted Maria to get Rob and Cher's phone number. I wanted to fly them out to Los Angeles to join us for this celebratory dinner. Francisco arranged for them to stay in a beautiful suite at *The Hotel 100*, and I arranged their flights and a limousine to pick them up from the airport, but this was the first time I was able to meet them face to face.

Rob was now in his mid-sixties. He was taller than I expected, though I had forgotten that he was a star point guard on his college basketball team at the *University of Hawaii*. He had light brown and silver hair, a silver goatee, and eyes as blue as Paul Newman's. When I shook his hand, he had a massively strong grip, yet his countenance exuded the same gentle kindness and warmth as Francisco's.

Cher was just as beautiful as Takeo had articulated. She was also tall in stature, as Rob was not the only athlete in their marriage. Cher was an *All-American* volleyball player when they met in college. In fact, before they even met, Rob saw a picture of her on the cover of her volleyball team's program, and he told one of his basketball teammates, "I'm going to marry that girl one day."

I guess Takeo wasn't the only one in the room with vision.

Cher's long, dark, flowing Hawaiian hair was pulled back in a loose ponytail and her smile had the kind of warmth that changed the temperature in the room. She wore an *Emilio Pucci* kaftan that I arranged to be waiting for her in their suite at *The Hotel 100*. I wanted to create a special evening for everyone, but especially for the Charlestons, for without them, there would be no Takeo.

Takeo was so excited to see them. He rushed over to give Cher a kiss on the cheek and an extra-long embrace. He had so much reverence for her and loved Cher as his big sister. Then he approached Rob. A deep Japanese bow, followed by an even longer embrace, came before his tears.

I then announced, "To everyone in this room, words cannot express the level of gratitude I have towards each and every one of you. You have each played such a significant role in my life, making me a better businessman, a better husband, a better father, a better student, a better teacher, and a better man. But most of all, you have each helped me discover who I really am, and I can honestly say that I no longer need to hide from myself."

Then Takeo politely interjected.

"Vincent, Maria and I wanted to get you a little something to commemorate this evening because we know how much you've been through," Takeo said, handing me a small box.

"Should I open it now?" I asked.

"If you like, sure," Takeo replied.

As I carefully opened the box that was meticulously wrapped in Japanese *washi* paper, I couldn't believe what was inside. It was a watch – a *Credor Eichi II* – but not just *any Eichi II*. It was *one of one*. It was the same as the one he wore on his wrist, with one exception.

He explained, "I wanted to do something special for you – something that embodied the work we've done together. I had this idea of breaking and repairing the porcelain dial using the *kintsugi* technique."

The brilliant white porcelain pieces had beautiful gold veins running through the cracks, highlighting the areas where the dial had broken, just like the *kintsugi* teacup Takeo had repaired in front of my own eyes.

"Vincent, this watch is *one of one*, just like you. It is imperfect, just like you, but its beauty is found in its imperfection, just like you. As you know, I read *The Icon Effect* the night before Francisco introduced us, and so I am very familiar with *Rule #25: Never Forget How God Sees You*. With all of our imperfections, God still loves us, and so as His children, we should also love each other with all of our imperfections. That is what true love is all about. I love you as a brother, and I am proud to have you and your family as part of my family," Takeo said, putting his arm around Maria and pulling her in close.

"Salud!" I exclaimed as we all toasted this momentous occasion.

As always, dinner at *Amor* was amazing, and it was an honor to sit next to Rob that evening as he shared many stories about Takeo's younger years with him in Hawaii.

"The first evening Takeo moved in with us, I took him to the driving range at this little nine-hole golf course by our house. He was using Cher's clubs and was struggling a bit, so I handed him one of my clubs to try," Rob said.

Takeo started laughing and chimed in.

"At first, I politely declined because Rob handed me his brand new driver he just bought a few weeks prior. I told him I was afraid of damaging it. Rob looked at me and said, *'What could possibly happen?'* And so on my first swing, the club head hit the turf mat about three inches before the ball, and the club head snapped off and went flying over the fence to the left of the tee box. I was standing there holding the club shaft in my hands with no club head, absolutely mortified!" Takeo said.

"But Takeo paid to have the club repaired. It was no big deal," Rob said.

"Vincent, it was his brand new driver!" exclaimed Takeo as he and Rob laughed uncontrollably.

It was such an inspiring thing to see these two men that had so much love and respect for one another dining at the same table as me and my family. I wanted so badly to contribute to someone else's life the way The Icon mentored me – the way Rob mentored Takeo – and the way Takeo mentored me. I wondered if that day would ever come.

Every void that was created in my life by someone leaving had been filled by a higher caliber person. I was now thankful for each betrayal, each hardship, and each gut-wrenching challenge, for they not only made me stronger, but they had opened voids that were filled by my new mentor, partner, and friend. Takeo created a shift in my life that only he could have.

This was *The Takeo Effect*.

Just then, our server walked into the room and approached me. He had a concerned look on his face.

"Mr. Montgomery, are you expecting another guest?"

"No. This is everyone right here," I replied.

"Sir, there's a man that says he needs to speak with you, and he made it sound like it was something urgent. Would you like me to escort him out, or would you like to speak with him?" our server asked.

I looked at Takeo and said, "Excuse me, let me go find out what this is all about. I'll be right back."

"Do you want me to come with you?" Takeo asked, looking concerned.

"Nah, it's cool. I'll handle it. It's probably nothing," I said.

As I walked to the front of the restaurant into the reception area, our server said, "There he is sir, the gentleman standing over there in the dark brown jacket."

As the gentleman turned around to face me, I couldn't believe it. He was not a *gentleman* at all.

It was Kane.

He approached me slowly and tentatively, saying, "Look Vincent, I know you probably hate me."

"Probably?" I responded.

"You have every right to. I ruined everything. I know it. Andrei put all these ideas in my head about you, and I couldn't see it back then. When the pandemic hit, our firm completely fell apart. Andrei walked away from our 7-year office lease and stuck me with $7.2 million in remaining rent. Plus, he's under investigation for insider trading because he and Michael started doing shady deals with the Russian mafia. Then he had to shut down his jewelry business because he owed some Armenian dudes a ton of money for a diamond shipment he never settled up. Vincent, I'm in bad shape – really bad shape. We had to dissolve our firm completely. I have nothing now," Kane confessed as he shuttered, unable to make direct eye contact with me.

I unbuttoned my coat jacket as I inhaled deeply, then slowly exhaled, remembering that I had forgiven Kane in one of my cleansing meditations with Takeo. At least that's what I claimed to have done. I felt like a hypocrite because in that moment of seeing Kane for the first time in well over a year, I still had such tremendous resentment towards him.

"Vincent, I just want things to go back to how they used to be. I made a huge mistake when I left you, and I see that now. Please. I'm begging you for another chance. I have nowhere else to go. I'll do anything. Please," Kane pleaded with me.

I remembered what Takeo had said about our *deal*. I had committed to pay it forward and teach someone the same *Bushidō* code Takeo had taught me for no personal gain in return.

Kane looked at me with a defeated look in his eyes, full of remorse for what he had done. Was this supposed to be his path to redemption? Was I supposed to be his mentor after all?

My head told me to do one thing, but my heart told me to do something else. I couldn't tell if Kane had truly changed, or if it was only his circumstances that had changed. There is a big difference between the two.

Kane then said, "I know I've cost you millions of dollars in damages, and I can't repay you all of it right now. I just don't have that kind of money, but I *promise* I'll make it up to you if you give me a chance! Please, Vincent! I give you my *word*!"

Just then, I felt someone behind me place their hand on my shoulder.

I slowly turned around to see who it was.

It was Andrei.

THE 7 VIRTUES OF BUSHIDŌ 武士道 CODE

1. **Gi 義 (Righteousness)**: Be acutely honest throughout your dealings with all people. Believe in justice, not from other people, but from yourself. To the true warrior, all points of view are deeply considered regarding honesty, justice and integrity. Warriors make a full commitment to their decisions.

2. **Yū 勇 (Courage)**: Hiding like a turtle in a shell is not living at all. A true warrior must have heroic courage. It is absolutely risky. It is living life completely, fully and wonderfully. Heroic courage is not blind. It is intelligent and strong.

3. **Jin 仁 (Benevolence)**: Through intense training and hard work, the true warrior becomes quick and strong. They are not as most people. They develop a power that must be used for good. They have compassion. They help their fellow men at every opportunity. If an opportunity does not arise, they go out of their way to find one.

4. **Rei 礼 (Respect)**: True warriors have no reason to be cruel. They do not need to prove their strength. Warriors are not only respected for their strength in battle, but also by their dealings with others. The true strength of a warrior becomes apparent during difficult times.

5. **Makoto 誠 (Honesty)**: When warriors say that they will perform an action, it is as good as done. Nothing will stop them from completing what they say they will do. They do not have to *give their word*. They do not have to *promise*. Speaking and doing are the same action.

6. **Meiyo 名誉 (Honor)**: Warriors have only one judge of honor and character, and this is themselves. Decisions they make and how these decisions are carried out are a reflection of who they truly are. You cannot hide from yourself.

7. **Chūgi 忠義 (Loyalty)**: Warriors are responsible for everything that they have done and everything that they have said and all of the consequences that follow. They are immensely loyal to all of those in their care. To everyone that they are responsible for, they remain fiercely true.

THE ICON EFFECT

HOW THE RIGHT MENTOR CAN CHANGE THE COURSE OF YOUR LIFE, FOREVER.

DARREN SUGIYAMA

A SEQUEL TO *THE ICON EFFECT*

THE TAKEO EFFECT

HOW A BILLIONAIRE SAMURAI WARRIOR SAVED MY LIFE…

DARREN SUGIYAMA

W W W . D A R R E N S U G I Y A M A . C O M

www.ingramcontent.com/pod-product-compliance
Lightning Source LLC
Chambersburg PA
CBHW061523020726
47502CB00006B/2198